To Stephanie Ta,

Follow Your Dreams!

PROJECT-00

Dow K

DOW KUMP

ENDEAVOR PUBLISHING
Huntington Beach, California

Published by

Endeavor Publishing
P.O. Box 7863
Huntington Beach, CA 92646

Copyright© 2005 Dow Kump

This is a work of fiction. The events described here are imaginary; the settings and characters are fictitious and not intended to represent specific places or living persons.

Library of Congress Cataloging-in-Publication Data

Cataloging-in-Publication Data is available from the Library of Congress

PROJECT-00/Dow Kump
Family Reading
Action/Adventure

ISBN 978-0-9743843-6-8

Printed in the United States of America

First Endeavor Publishing Printing: November, 2003

20 19 18 17 16 15 14 13 12 11

www.dowkump.com

To Laura,

my choice companion

and best friend.

My love for you is eternal.

ACKNOWLEDGEMENTS

I would like to express my sincere gratitude to everyone who worked with me over the years in making this book possible. My thanks to illustrators Brian Murray and Eric Keawekane for creating impressive cover art; to my editors, Judith Ross Enderle and Stephanie Jacob Gordon of Writers Ink, who worked with me to tell a structured story; and to my formatter Gene Toth, who took my manuscript and made it shine. And, last of all, a special thanks to my friend, freelance editor Marc Feickert, who helped me round out the story and make it all come together. To all, your work will always be appreciated.

YOU HAVE NOT FAILED

UNTIL YOU QUIT TRYING.

GORDON B. HINCKLEY

PROJECT-00

The Wish

"Let it rip, Eric!"

Ooing and ahhing, five guys from my freshman class huddled around me as I pulled from a box my latest invention—a homemade, launchable, 12-inch space shuttle. Thanks to Dad's power tools it was ready to go, and we were T-minus thirty seconds to liftoff.

"Why did we have to come here?" one of the guys asked.

"You'll see," I said, as we stood by our high school swimming pool. My launch platform was an old Boogie board that I'd found in the attic, and had cut down to a 10-inch square piece. I carefully placed the space shuttle on it and gently pushed the Boogie board out into the deep end. I nodded, signaling everyone to start the countdown.

"Three . . . two . . . one . . . blastoff!" everyone shouted as I hit the button on my handheld remote. The space shuttle shook, hummed, and rattled, then released a cloud of white smoke from its boosters.

The blastoff was so powerful that it doused us with water, just like a twenty-foot, ten-ton whale at Sea World that slam dunks into the water from a fifteen-foot drop. All the guys cheered, excited by the spray.

Up into the cloudless sky my space shuttle soared. I showed off my astronaut flight skills and performed a few tricky loop-the-loops. I grinned from ear to ear. I couldn't help but marvel at my accomplishment.

"Guys, if you think that was cool, watch this!" I beamed with anticipation. I maneuvered my shuttle into a nosedive and cut the engines.

"Eric, it's gonna crash!" my friend yelled.

I hit a button on the remote, and two heartbeats later, a four-foot red-white-and-blue parachute blossomed from the tail of the shuttle. Instantly, in a controlled descent, the space shuttle floated to earth, just missed the diving board, and went SPLAT into the pool. All the guys went crazy, cheering, shaking me as if I had scored the winning touchdown at our homecoming game.

The school bell rang, and playtime was over. I reached out with the ten-foot pool hook and I pulled my shuttle and the Boogie board to the side. I quickly boxed them up and dashed to my gym locker to store them. When I looked up at the clock, I saw that I was late for my speech class and I charged out from the locker room and zipped down the hall.

I had just stepped inside my classroom when

my teacher, Mrs. Freederman, called on me to deliver my final speech of the year. I was unprepared. I had to think fast. I walked to the front of the class and cleared my throat, ready to let my imagination get me out of this predicament. The wheels in my head cranked full-on under the pressure, and presto—my brain found a story. I looked at the class and began:

"After baseball practice I rode my bike home and went to the fridge. Mom left me a note to microwave my dinner and then clean my room. I wasn't hungry so I decided to clean my room first.

"I started with my messy closet, tossing out a pile of old Halloween costumes I had worn over the years. When I pulled them out, a horrible smell almost knocked me out. It was the worst odor on this planet. I sniffed my costumes, but the awful stench wasn't in any of them. I chucked the costumes onto my bed and kept searching deeper in my closet, determined to find out what smelled so bad.

"While I was pulling out some dirty clothes that failed to land in my hamper, I came across my old baseball cleats from when I was six years old. To my surprise, I discovered a crusty old sock that was in my left shoe for seven years. The sock was once white, but now yellow, and mold was all over it.

"The smell was so terrible I decided to put it in the trash outside right away. I was about to walk out of the room, with my arm fully extended, holding the sock with my right hand, and plugging my nose with the other hand.

"When I reached the door, I heard a faint moan. I jerked around, and my mouth fell open with fright! Something out of this world happened. One of my costumes mysteriously came to life. A five-foot-tall mummy was reaching out to grab me. A huge scream leaped from my throat. I darted from my room shouting, 'HHHHHHHEELP!'

"The mummy chased after me. It moaned, and got closer, even though it limped. I sprinted outside and I headed straight to my tree house to hide.

"WHAM! I slammed the door shut, shaking from head to toe. 'Oh no! What a dumb move that was, Eric! Now you're trapped!' I said to myself, trembling. I could hear the mummy groaning, getting closer and closer.

"What should I do? What could I do? I was frantic!

"All of a sudden, it hit me. It was the only thing I could do to save my life. Once the mummy ripped open the door, it came directly toward me with outstretched arms. Just when it was inches away from my shaking body, the only thing I could do for self-defense was rub the stinky sock in its nose. The mummy took in a whiff and its eyes shot wide open. It stumbled backward and fell out of the tree house to the ground, then got up wailing and hobbled down the street. I owe it all to my Pee Wee baseball sock that saved the day.

"The End."

All the kids in my class laughed their heads off. One girl laughed so hard she got the hiccups. I looked to the back of the class at Mrs. Freederman, who had her arms crossed. She was not laughing or smiling. "Very funny, Eric Thomas. The speech assignment was to tell a *true*, three-minute story, about your worst chore at home."

I paused and said, "Well, cleaning my room is my worst chore."

"Take your seat. After school, go to the principal's office," Mrs. Freederman snapped.

Slumping into my chair, I had a sinking feeling that I was headed for big trouble. I figured things were slightly in my favor since it was the last day of school. But then I had a terrible thought: Mrs. Freederman might fail me. Things weren't looking good for my final report card.

All day I was scared about what was going to happen. The bell rang, school was over, and I walked to the principal's office with a weight in my stomach. Before I sat down Mr. Jordan said, "I saw your shuttle launch from the pool. Impressive!"

He then settled back into his leather chair and looked directly at me. "You're a very gifted boy, Eric. Where do you get your bright imagination—from your mom or your dad?"

"Neither," I replied. "I think it's from the cereal I'm eating."

Mr. Jordan cracked a cool smile and let a little laugh slip from his lips. He then picked up a file and pulled out a manila folder. "I reviewed your school records today and I didn't know you skipped the seventh grade. You went straight from the sixth grade to the eighth grade."

"My teacher said I was ready and academically capable to advance a year," I said.

Mr. Jordan then picked up my report card and nodded. "Four A's and three B's. That's a successful freshman year. The only trouble was being late so many times to Mrs. Freederman's speech class. Why?"

"Well, every morning before school, I'm always tinkering with some gadget in the garage and lose track of time. I promise never to be late next year. Not one day."

"Mrs. Freederman told me that you need to develop more self-discipline with regards to school assignments and recommended that you attend summer school."

Summer school . . . oh no, I thought, shaking my head.

"Eric, you're a good student, and you promised not to be late next year. Do you keep your promises?"

"I do," I said quickly and firmly.

"Honesty is a great quality. You show me a person who's honest, and I'll show you a person with self-discipline. Do you know who said that?"

I paused, thinking of great presidents. "Abraham Lincoln?" I guessed.

"No, my mother," Mr. Jordan countered as he chuckled, revealing his funny side. I laughed with him and he continued. "In my fifty-two years of living, I've discovered she's right. Now, Eric, next year I'm counting on you not to have tardy marks. I will convince Mrs. Freederman you do not need summer school. But if you are consistently late next year—you will attend."

I sighed in great relief, and I put my hand out and shook Mr. Jordan's. "Deal."

Mr. Jordan got up, opened the door, and gave me my report card. "You're very clever. I wouldn't be surprised if on your summer vacation your imagination gets you into some big adventure."

"Cool." I grinned.

"Have any trips planned?" Mr. Jordan asked.

"My uncle is a marine biologist, and he travels all over the world in his triple-decker yacht, studying underwater life. He's taking me and my older brother on his boat on the Pacific Ocean to some remote islands to help him perform some experiments. It's going to be a blast," I said.

"Sounds exciting," Mr. Jordan said.

I then flashed him two thumbs up and charged out the door. Rushing to my locker, I gathered the box holding my space shuttle and the Boogie board and began my trip home. Along the way, I kept thinking about what Mr. Jordan had said about my clever imagination. *So where do I get it from?*

I felt a lot of it had to do with the dinky town where I lived—San Andreas. It was in Northern California. The population was a freckle over a thousand people. It had one barber shop, two banks, a doughnut shop, a gas station, two grocery stores, and a post office. Life in San Andreas was pretty much boringville. To survive, a kid like me had to use his creative ability. I guess that was where I got my fully developed imagination. I was always thinking up something to make in the garage to keep myself entertained. But even though life in San Andreas was on the dull side, it was home, and I wouldn't want to live anywhere else in the world.

As I approached my house, I came to a sudden halt when a Frisbee bonked me in the forehead.

"Hey, Eric. Way to use your head for a backstop," a voice teased. I looked around and spotted my fifteen-year-old brother, Buzz, behind a tree in a park. He was doubled over laughing at his joke.

"Very funny," I shouted rubbing my head. "Why'd you do that?"

"Easy target."

I shook my head, wondering how we could be brothers. We were such complete opposites. I was tall and skinny with blond wavy hair. A handful of freckles dotted my nose and cheeks. But Buzz was short and chubby with brown hair. Being clever, I gave him the family nickname Buzz—because every time he went to the barber, he would get a buzz cut. Buzz had zero imagination and he failed miserably in attempting to be clever at giving me a nickname—Technobrain. Too long, too boring, too dull.

Buzz met up with me, and we walked home together. I didn't say a word, giving him the cold shoulder. After a few minutes, Buzz said, "Hey, look." He pointed at one of our neighbors, Mr. Anderson, who was hammering a yard sale sign onto a telephone pole. "Let's go see what kind of junk he's selling."

We went through the gate to Mr. Anderson's yard and I put my boxed-up space shuttle and the Boogie board on a table.

"Tomorrow's the big sale. See anything you want, boys?" Mr. Anderson asked.

We fumbled through a box that had a worn-out iron, a lampshade, a pair of size-ten bowling shoes, and a stinky baseball glove. Buzz rolled his eyes and mumbled, "Ho-hum, let's go."

As we turned to leave, I saw something sparkle and spotted a jar of coins. One of the coins was shining more brightly than the rest—it had been the one to catch my attention. I picked up the jar, which contained three old foreign coins—one I recognized was from Mexico.

"Hey, what's the story with these coins, Mr. Anderson?" I asked.

"Found the jar in the attic. Have no idea where it came from. Pick one for free. More than that, you'll have to pay."

I fished out the coin I wanted, the sparkling yellow coin, and examined it. There was a picture of an open treasure chest full of gold. Inscribed under the treasure chest were three words: *Make a wish.*

I showed it to Buzz. He shrugged and muttered, "Big deal. It's just a coin from some cheap carnival. Besides, I don't believe in wishes. They're just fairy tales that don't come true."

"I agree, but if wishes did come true, know what I'd wish for?"

"What?"

"One million dollars."

"One million bucks. You'd split it with me, right?" Buzz said, putting his arm around my shoulder.

"Fat chance. You bonked me in the head with a Frisbee."

"Hey, that's what little brothers are for—to pick on."

I put the coin in my pocket, grabbed the boxed-up space shuttle, and out the gate we went to go home.

In our backyard Mom and Dad were preparing a barbecue. Just as I put everything on the table next to a bowl of potato chips, I heard a soft bark. I looked down and it was Pugsly, our playful Labrador. I gave him a chip and went over to Dad, who was lighting the coals.

"School's out. Bet you feel like a million bucks," Dad said.

Million bucks . . . funny that Buzz and I were just

talking money, I thought, looking at the fire flickering on the coals. "Yep, a million bucks all right."

Dad settled in a lawn chair and picked up the sports page. I pulled the sparkling yellow coin from my pocket. Reading the words *Make a wish*, I let my imagination wander. *A million bucks . . . that's a lot of homemade inventions*, I thought as I stared into the yellow flames.

"Eric, back up, you're too close to the fire," Mom said as she set a plate of hamburgers on the table. Moving one step backward, I continued thinking about a million dollars. *That's some serious cash.* Then my brain shifted gears and I thought of birthday wishes. Ever since I could remember, before I would huff and puff and blow out the candles on my cake, I'd make a wish. It was some tradition that started somewhere, and it happened on birthdays, young or old.

This was not my birthday, but it was the perfect occasion to celebrate: School was out for ninety-five glorious days, and that made me want to make a wish with my new coin. I glanced up to see if anyone was watching. Nope. Buzz was stuffing his face with potato chips, Dad was still reading the sports page, and Mom was slicing tomatoes for the hamburgers. I lifted my fist, squeezed my eyes shut, and made my wish. *I want one million bucks . . . I'll accept a check or a lump sum of cash, but no credit cards.* I snickered to myself, enjoying my goofy sense of humor.

I opened my eyes, satisfied with my wish, and

flipped the coin in the air. When I reached out to snag it, my finger hit the coin and it landed in the barbecue.

"My cool coin!" I gasped, looking at it on top of the hot coals. Right then, a wild blaze shot straight up, roaring six feet high.

"AHHHHHHHHHHHH!" I screamed, leaping backward. The fire blazed like I had poured a bucket of gasoline on the coals.

"WHAT IN THE WORLD!" Dad shouted, throwing the sports page down. He rushed for the garden hose. Frightened, Mom flung tomatoes into the air, and darted towards me exclaiming, "OH MY GOSH!"

In the commotion, Pugsly was barking continuously while Buzz was the only one to remain calm. He sat there grinning, licking potato chips from his fingers. "Cool!"

I was stunned, not knowing how all this had happened, except that it was from the coin. *Amazing,* I thought, taking it all in with raised eyebrows that had narrowly escaped being singed off. I looked at the billowing flames, and at that moment a spine-tingling chill went down my back. A huge grin then inched across my face. I felt that something extraordinary was about to happen! Was my million-dollar wish going to come true?

Disaster

The next day I plopped myself out of bed and stretched. It was Saturday—my favorite day of the week. And with school out, every day was now the weekend. I got dressed and went to the garage to tinker with one of my latest projects. It had been twenty-four weeks in the making, and now it was time for the big test run. Leaning over my worktable, I reached into a bag and grabbed a handful of my favorite treats: Marshmallows. Zero nutrition for breakfast, but there was nothing like a tasty treat to get the day started. As I munched, enjoying every bite, I put my hand in my pocket, felt my coin, and pulled it out. The edges were melted and it had black stains from the charcoal. Even though it looked so bad, I could still see the treasure chest.

I shoved the coin back into my pocket and turned back to my invention, gazing at it with pride. Its code name was so top secret, I was the only one who knew it: *Commando.* He was a mobile five-foot robot made from a couple of buckets of bolts, tin, wiring, computer chips, and Duracell batteries. Mom said he looked like a knight in shining armor.

While gazing at him, I felt something rub against my leg. I looked down and was greeted by big brown eyes. It was Pugsly, wagging his tail, begging to snack on my marshmallows.

"Here boy, want one?" I asked as I rubbed his ears.

Excited, Pugsly ate the marshmallow I offered wagging his tail faster and faster. Having done that, it was time to focus on the task at hand: programming Commando to do one of my chores. I opened his stomach to reveal the primary input and output wires hooked to a battery power pack. There were also hundreds of mini buttons, switches, knobs, and flashing colored lights. As I inspected Commando's home-made guts, I could hear Pugsly sniffing the metal feet. I began to work Commando's controls, playing with buttons and knobs, making his eyes blink green like some kind of alien from Mars.

I closed his stomach, took the remote control off the table, and maneuvered him closer and closer to Dad's riding power lawnmower. I opened the garage door and positioned Commando on the seat. His movements were jerky, but I got his hands to start the motor and put it into gear.

Concentrating, I controlled Commando's right foot, put on a little more gas, and out he zipped from the garage onto the lawn. *Perfect,* I said to myself. I did it! Kids in the neighborhood were watching and pointing as I controlled Commando, making him mow the lawn. "It works, Pugsly! Dad's not going to believe this in a million years!"

Pugsly barked and wagged his tail.

"Cool stuff, Eric!" one kid yelled, giving me a thumbs-up.

Using the remote, I controlled Commando's arms and sent the lawnmower back and forth across the lawn.

"Hey, boy genius, get that thing to do all my home-work next year!" Buzz shouted, walking out from the garage.

As usual, I ignored Buzz and went about cutting green blades of grass. Everything was working like a charm until a strange popping sound came from Commando. It was like popcorn kernels exploding in a microwave. *Pop. Pop. Pop.* The sounds kept getting louder with each pop.

"Sounds like your bucket of bolts has some screws loose, just like inside your head." Buzz chuckled.

Frustrated, I worked the controls, flipping switches to try to shut Commando down, but it was no use, his eyes flashed on and off like Christmas lights. There was no way to get him under control. Right then a panic button went off inside my brain!

"Something's wrong!" I gasped, beginning to panic.

A split second later, the worst thing happened. One of the buttons on the remote jammed, and Commando's foot pressed down harder on the gas pedal. The mower zoomed off the lawn, broke down our picket fence, and charged onto the street. A loud screech echoed throughout the neighborhood as tires burned rubber.

Commando was out of control. I flew after him, and all I could hear was the roaring laughter from my friends. Buzz was the loudest. "WAY TO GO, GENIUS!"

What a disaster, I thought as my robot swerved the mower all over the place.

WHAM! Commando wiped out six mailboxes, took out Mrs. Johnson's prized rose garden, and demolished a stop sign. I kept hitting the jammed controller but it was stuck tight.

Commando was now heading for a huge, oak tree. I shook the remote and smacked it with my hand and the jammed button finally popped out. Twisting knobs, I somehow got control of Commando's arms and caused him to swerve away from the tree at the last possible second. Sweat drenched me as I watched Dad's lawnmower almost get crunched. Pugsly was barking his head off, keeping up with me, as we chased my robot. Finally gaining on Commando, I watched his stomach burst open then shoot out red and white sparks, burnt springs, coils, and sizzling red-hot wires.

"Oh no!" I wailed.

Seconds later, a police car with flashing red lights and a blaring siren whipped around the corner.

Spending the summer behind bars wasn't my idea of a cool summer vacation. Panting and running, I clutched the remote. Commando zoomed into an alley. Ahead of us, a painter in white overalls was standing on top of a fifteen-foot ladder. Commando was barreling straight for him. I twisted the knob which controlled his arms, but I was too late.

SMACK! He shattered the ladder as he whizzed by. The painter grasped the window ledge, hanging on for his life. Glancing back, I saw the police hot on my trail. The painter struggled to climb into the window and knocked a few gallons of paint off the ledge. WHAM! The cops' windshield was plastered with blue, green, and yellow paint. The police car slammed into a row of garbage bins, shooting trash all over the place.

With my palms wet from cold sweat pouring down my armpits, I dropped the remote. Quickly picking it up, I saw for the first time, Commando's foot ease up on the gas.

"YES!" I cheered.

Tired and out of breath, I maneuvered Commando back home and brought him to an abrupt stop in the garage. Just when I thought it couldn't get any worse, Commando blew his main fuse, shooting flames from his tin body into the air. I scrambled for Dad's fire extinguisher and put out my blazing robot. Buzz stood in the doorway, laughing the whole time.

"What a great show that was, Eric." Buzz said,

stuffing a dollar bill in my shirt pocket. "Next time charge admission in the neighborhood, and you'll get rich!"

Discouraged, I gazed at my robot. White smoke came out of his ears. Looking at Dad's destroyed lawnmower, I knew that I was in deep, deep trouble.

In the living room with Pugsly, I flopped on the couch. I stared at the floor, wondering how I was going to explain this to Mom and Dad. Worried, petting Pugsly, I was wishing that the accident had never, ever happened. I then wondered if there was a way to change wishes. I'd trade my million-dollar wish for not getting grounded for life any day. Pugsly licked my hand, feeling sorry for his master.

Then, Mom and Dad came in from the backyard.

"What's the matter?" Dad asked.

Oh boy, the moment of truth. I cleared my throat and announced, "Um, I made a little blunder."

"Did your knight in shining armor blow up the garage?" Mom asked jokingly.

Inside I was thinking, *Run away from home, Eric. Just fly out that door and don't look back.* With butterflies in my stomach, I dropped the big bomb and told them what had happened. Their eyes kept growing wider and wider. They ran out to the garage, and were shocked by the sight of my burnt robot slumped over the lawnmower and white fire extinguisher foam sprayed everywhere. I was so scared that I was shaking in my sneakers.

It was a gut-wrenching experience watching Dad slowly circle the scene, looking at the sizzled-up robot on his smashed lawnmower. He put his hands on his hips and with a deep, stern voice barked, "Every dime of your life savings is going to pay for these damages, Eric! The mailboxes, the stop sign, the fence, and my lawnmower. And I have no idea what we're going to do to get Mrs. Johnson to forgive you for wiping out her prized rose garden."

I released the biggest sigh of my life, wanting no more than to crawl in a deep black hole and not come out for a long, long time . . . twenty-six sounded like a good age. I nodded at Dad, slumped over, stuffed my hands deep in my pockets, and headed to my room. I fell onto my bed and stared up at the ceiling. I felt like the biggest, dumbest loser in the world.

Buzz interrupted my thoughts. He looked down at me, grinning from ear to ear as he ate a doughnut.

"Guess it's back to the old drawing board, huh, sport?"

"There's no back to the drawing board because I quit! I'm never going to make anything else as long as I live."

Mom poked her head into the room. "Did I hear you say 'quit'?"

"Yep, that's Eric, Mr. Quitter," Buzz mumbled, stuffing the rest of the doughnut in his mouth.

"Buzz, leave!" Mom said firmly.

Buzz smirked, then trudged off. Mom gently closed

the door and sat on the edge of the bed. "Eric . . . a quitter. Some of the greatest inventors of our time failed hopelessly."

"Did any of them wipe out a prized rose garden, mow down a row of mailboxes, and destroy a lawn-mower, only to become bankrupt paying for repairs?" I fired back.

Mom kept her cool. By the sound of my voice she knew I was discouraged. Rubbing my hand she said, "You've got this fun, creative brain, and every time you tackle something and see it backfire on the first attempt, you give up and mope. Do you have any idea how many great inventors have failed on their first attempt?"

"Ah, save the speech, Mom. I'm not in the mood. All my savings are gone."

But Mom didn't stop. She told me I should keep working on my robot and perfect it and sell it to kids around town or on the Internet. "What kid wouldn't want a robot to do his least favorite chores around the house? And it would be a way to make some money."

When she mentioned money, I thought of my wish again—one million dollars. *Wow, she's really onto something.*

Mom added that anything can be accomplished with good old-fashioned, gritty determination. She told me the story about Thomas Edison, who invented the phonograph and the light bulb. She told me how that great inventor had many failures, frustrations, and disappointments, but he stuck to his ideas until he achieved success.

Mom was getting me to perk up. *Keep going,* I thought. I felt her pep talk working. It gave me a warm feeling in my heart, and I remembered the time I gave Mom a clay flower pot I made for Mother's Day. It turned out pretty cruddy, but when I put a flower in it and gave it to her, she smiled and gave me a big hug and kiss and said it was the best gift in the world. That was the kind of warm feeling I had.

Mom then reminded me about Buzz, how during his freshman year the coach didn't think he was a good enough tackler and cut him from the football team. Instead of becoming discouraged, Buzz was determined to make the team the following year and spent hours of persistent practice tackling a homemade scarecrow. Every day he would run and slam into the scarecrow in the backyard until its head would pop off. Doing that every day made him better and when tryouts came the following year, he made the team and helped his squad win a local championship, gaining a reputation as "Mr. Tough-As-Nails."

I was getting the picture loud and clear and nodded my head up and down like a puppet. Mom picked up a football from the floor and started to play catch with me. Back and forth across the room we tossed the old pigskin. Mom then said something that really hit me in the gut: "Nothing great will ever happen without determination." I froze for a moment, thinking hard about it. I tucked the football under my arm and flopped down in a beanbag. Mom moved out the door, leaving me staring at the carpet.

It was at that moment, thinking about what Mom had said, that my attitude changed. I got up feeling I could triumph at whatever I tackled. I was ready to conquer the world. *From here on out, no matter how big the obstacle, I'm not giving up easily—mark my words!*

CHAPTER THREE

The Mission

A beam of sunlight shined through my window, nailing me between the eyes. I woke up in a good mood from a solid night's sleep, ready to put the previous day's disaster behind me. Energized, I went through my morning routine of getting dressed, combing my hair, and brushing my teeth. I opened a desk drawer and pulled out the shoebox that contained my life's savings. *Time to hand it over,* I said to myself, ready to pay for the damages Commando had done.

I gazed at the sea of green cash that filled the box. Five hundred bucks. Some I'd earned from good grades and doing odd jobs around the house, but most had come from working at the family business during the Christmas season. We owned a Christmas tree farm called Needles Point, and everyone in the county came each year to buy their Christmas trees from us. Sometimes I would tell my teachers that if they would up my grades, I'd lower the price; some years it worked, most years it didn't.

My parents had owned the farm for twenty years, since they were first married. We had one-hundred acres of trees, and I could tell you the difference between a Douglas Fir and a Norway Spruce without a book. My favorite tree was the "Cadillac" of Christmas trees, the Fraser Fir. It's a tall tree with short needles and a great woodsy smell.

As I was about to enter the living room, I noticed Mom and Dad at the kitchen table. Dad was slumped in his chair with his elbows on his knees, staring at the floor. *Something's wrong,* I thought. *Something's very wrong.*

Tears rolled down Mom's cheeks. I froze, my ears perked up. I waited and listened to Mom's faint voice quiver as she said, "I can't deal with the thought of losing our family business!"

What in the world! We're losing our Christmas tree farm? What is going on here? I wondered, completely stunned. They didn't say anything else for a long moment. Cat-like, I cautiously peeked at my parents.

"I can't believe it. This is the worst thing that has ever happened to us. Are you sure the broken irrigation system will be a million dollars to repair? Mom asked.

"Yes," answered Dad. "I got the second estimate in the mail this morning. And if we don't get it fixed by the end of summer, one-hundred acres of Christmas trees will die without water, and dead Christmas trees don't sell."

"What are we going to do?" Mom moaned.

"I'll keep trying to get the money, but so far all the banks I've tried won't loan us the money because of our past credit problems. I'm afraid we might be forced to sell the farm."

Mom kept shaking her head. I felt sick. We couldn't lose our farm! Losing it would be like not having Christmas! By this time I was feeling pretty crummy.

"Let's not breathe a word of this to the boys," Dad mumbled. "I don't want them to worry."

Worry? I was freaking out! Losing our Christmas tree farm would be a huge bummer. I felt I had taken a punch to my stomach. I took a deep breath and counted to ten. The best thing would be to play it cool and act like I hadn't heard a thing. I walked into the kitchen and handed Dad my shoebox.

"Here's all my money to pay for the damages. I promise this will never happen again."

Mom had wiped her eyes and gave me a warm smile, as if she was telling me it wasn't the end of the world.

"Learn anything from this?" Dad grumbled.

"Sure did. Next time I'm going to have my robot take out the trash. Much safer."

Mom winked at me. Dad rolled his eyes, got up from the table, and moved to the window. He looked out, not saying a word.

"Go outside, Eric. Your father and I are in the middle of something," Mom said.

I nodded and darted out the door. In the backyard I eased myself into our hammock. Looking up into the clear blue sky, I was still stunned from the news I'd overheard. I wanted to tell Buzz, but he was a big, fat blabbermouth. He couldn't keep a secret if his life depended on it.

"Hmmm," I uttered, as I swayed back and forth and let my imagination wander in any direction that would lead me to my pot of gold under the rainbow. What could I do to get the money to save our farm? *Commando.* If only he worked, I could quite possibly sell him to a toy company, and presto—we'd be in the money, and Mom's and Dad's worries would be over.

I smirked, crossing my arms, knowing this wasn't the winning idea. How long would it take me to get Commando perfected? Could take six months or longer. We didn't have that much time. Strike one.

What about selling the idea for my mini space shuttle that I launched from the school pool? What kid wouldn't want to goof off with that? Pondering that idea, I came to the conclusion that it wasn't the winning idea, either. The biggest obstacle against me was time. Tomorrow, Buzz and I would take off with our Uncle for our big two-month ocean trip. I wanted to go so bad, but now all I wanted to do was spend my summer vacation getting the money our family needed to save the farm. I racked my brain, but nothing would come to me.

For some reason I kept hearing the words that

Mom had said to me: *Nothing great will ever happen without determination.*

I was a new kid now, determined to succeed at whatever I put my mind to.

I was definitely determined to use my keen imagination to save our Christmas tree farm. The problem was, what else could I do? I was stumped—not a good sign.

I got up from the hammock and hoped that if I did some pushups, it would get my blood pumping in my brain, make sparks fly, and I would have a creative moment. After about a dozen, I noticed a pair of size-ten sneakers standing in front of me.

"What are you doing?" Buzz snickered.

"Oh . . . I'm . . . getting in shape to fix my robot," I said, huffing and puffing.

"Mom's little pep talk sure did wonders for you," Buzz mumbled, walking into the house.

"Twenty-six . . . twenty-seven . . . come on, brain," I exhaled.

Running out of steam, after my thirtieth pushup, I rolled onto my back hoping that it had done the trick. As I looked up at the sky, thoughts flashed through my brain. I could see that strange treasure chest coin and I had a freaky feeling that my million-dollar wish was going to come true . . . yet it was a mystery as to how and when it would happen. I'd always loved mysteries, but this one had me fooled. Or maybe I was just fooling myself.

Pugsly snapped me out of my thoughts by licking my face for some friendly attention from his master. I stroked Pugs under his ears, and while I looked into his brown eyes something hit me.

"Treasure! Ideas are flowing my furry friend!"

An idea was stirring. In a school report I had done in my history class, I had written about how pirates had terrorized the sea from the 1600s to the 1700s, a time period called the Golden Age of Piracy. During that time, pirates like Black Beard and One-Eyed Jack would attack European ships loaded with supplies and steal all their gold, food, and clothing.

In my research, I found out that a French pirate ship had been discovered off the coast of Florida by a team of oceanographers. Inside the sunken ship they found six million dollars worth of treasure. That thought made my heart accelerate . . . I was onto something! I dug deeper into my memory, recalling a group of pirates who traveled the Pacific Ocean near Ticonderoga Island. They wanted to hide their stolen treasure there, but their ship caught fire and sank. It was believed that ten million dollars of treasure was on board, and to this day no one had discovered it.

Grinning, I knew I had the winning idea. This was awesome—everything was falling into my hands. All I had to do was get my uncle to go where the pirate ship was last seen and let us search using his underwater equipment. It was a long shot, but I believed we could discover that ship, take hold of the treasure, and become rich. I remembered what Mr. Jordan had told me about my imagination. It certainly was going to get me into some big-league adventure over summer vacation.

"Done deal," I told Pugsly. "And don't worry, boy, when your master gets back, no more dog bones for you—steak!" He barked, liking that idea.

Now that my game plan was set, there was something important that I needed to do. Whispering, I told Pugs that it was a top-secret mission and that every secret mission needed a code name, like the military used. Wacky, goofy code names floated in my brain. Then, something cool struck me. Since we needed a whole bunch of money, that could mean only one thing. *How many zeros are in a million? Six. I have the perfect name for my mission.*

"PROJECT-000000," I said to Pugsly. He didn't bark, wag his tail, or jump up and down. "Um, I think my secret code name is too long. How about PROJECT-00?" He wagged his tail and barked three times. That was a great sign. Pugsly liked the code name. It was a winner.

Having named my mission, I was ready to get to work. I knew it was a long shot, but nothing great would ever happen if I didn't try.

I glanced at my watch and realized it was time to get packed for the big trip. Early in the morning Mom and Dad would drive Buzz and me to San Francisco to meet my uncle at his yacht. From there, we would set sail for the biggest ocean adventure of my life. Now, more than ever, I was excited, because I had a strong feeling that my plan might work. What could possibly go wrong?

Full Speed Ahead

The following morning, shortly after eight o'clock, I shot out of bed excited to head for San Francisco. I think I set a new kid's world record for making my bed, getting dressed, brushing my teeth, combing my hair, and lacing up my sneakers—forty-six seconds.

I dashed to the kitchen where Mom was dishing up golden brown pancakes and Buzz was pouring orange juice.

"The van is packed," Dad said, walking in from the garage.

"Great, let's have breakfast," Mom said cheerfully.

I wolfed my pancakes down.

"Slow down," Dad cried.

"I can't. I can't wait to go on the trip!"

"Me too," Buzz said, gulping down his orange juice.

"How long will it take to get to San Francisco?" I mumbled through a mouthful of pancakes.

"Three hours," Mom replied.

Three hours, that's a lot of time for daydreaming.

Leaning back in my chair, I rubbed my full stomach and licked some maple syrup from my lips. Boy, I felt that I had broken another kid's world record. *This one would be for speed eating,* I thought, chuckling to myself. If only I knew how to drive. With the way I was breaking records, we'd zip to San Francisco in no time.

"Honey, you were a sailor in the Navy," Mom said to Dad, finishing the last pancake. "Give the boys some advice in case they get sick to their stomachs out on the ocean."

Dad looked up from his morning newspaper. "If you feel seasick and have the urge to hurl, make sure there isn't a strong wind blowing against you when you puke over the side of the boat. I made that mistake once and ended up wearing my lunch all day."

Buzz and I laughed, enjoying Dad's tip. Mom shook her head. I got up and went outside. The air was crisp, birds were singing, and there wasn't a cloud in the sky. My mind started to drift, and I reflected on our Christmas tree farm. Every summer, Buzz and I worked with Dad for hours, trimming acres of trees so they would be full and perfectly shaped when Christmas arrived. I felt sad knowing, for the first time, I would not be around to help Dad trim the trees. I gave myself a little pep talk so I wouldn't feel so sad. *When I get home from Project-00, I will be the hero of the family, all because I dared to tackle the impossible. And if it weren't for Mr. Anderson's yard sale, I never would have found that strange coin, and the million-dollar wish never would have happened.* I pulled the sizzled coin from my pocket. I could still picture the magical moment the coin landed on the hot coals sending roaring flames dancing in the air. Never would I forget the feeling that overcame me. The wish I desired could possibly come true.

My thoughts were interrupted as the others came out.

"Let's go," Dad said.

I put the coin in my pocket as we all got into the van. In a jiff we were officially off, heading to San Francisco.

Cruising down the road, Dad turned on the radio and tuned into some boring radio talk show. Buzz looked at me and rolled his eyes. He then put on his headphones, turned on his portable CD player and cranked the sound full blast so he could rock out to his favorite group, The Screaming Hornets. Mom pulled out her reading glasses and opened her latest mystery novel.

While everyone was doing their own things, I pulled out a pocket-sized map of the Pacific Ocean. As I rubbed Pugsly's ears, my eyes scanned the map, searching for the tropical island where the pirate ship had sunk. I was surprised at all the tiny islands in the ocean. It took a long time, but I finally found the island I was looking for. Bingo! My eyes zeroed in on the island of Ticonderoga. *Yes, that's the place where all the loot is.*

I leaned my head back on the seat. I closed my eyes and pictured myself in a mini-submarine searching the ocean floor for the sunken pirate ship. Colorful fish swam past the submarine, and an octopus with long slithery tentacles floated around. As I maneuvered the imaginary submarine, I was discouraged at not finding the pirate ship. I told myself, *I can't quit. Finding treasure in the ocean is never easy and often risky with the man-eating sharks. No matter how great the odds are against me, I have to keep going. I can't let my family down. More than ever I want to go home and be the family hero for finding the treasure and saving our Christmas tree farm.*

Sweat poured down my face as I realized that I was lost in the depths of the sea. My vision had become blurred by the blackness of the water, but I was determined and pressed onward. As I kept going, the dark water started to become clear. In the far distance, I saw a ship.

Excitedly, I worked my way toward it and discovered a rusty cannon barrel sticking out from its side. I circled overhead and spotted a treasure chest on the top deck. My heart beat faster and faster. I knew that this was what the feeling would be like when I found the real treasure chest. I lowered the submarine next to the chest and the lid popped open. I gasped, gazing at the chest full of gold coins.

Satisfied, I sighed and opened my eyes. Pugsly was fast asleep on my lap. I gazed out the window at the smooth, rolling hills as we cruised down the country road. Sunshine beaming through the window felt good on my face. After gazing at the train tracks that ran beside the highway for a long time, my eyelids became heavier and heavier, which meant snooze time. That was okay; it made time go by faster. I closed my eyes, again knowing that when Buzz jabbed me we would be in San Francisco.

As I slept, warm beads of sweat rolled down my forehead. My eyes flickered when I felt a solid punch on my right shoulder.

"Hey, wake up, we're here," Buzz said.

My eyes flew open, and I sat straight up. My neck was sore from the slumped position I'd been in, but who cared. I was in the big city and soon I'd be with my uncle on his boat. Rubbing my neck, I looked out the window toward the city. I saw that there was a low cover of fog gently resting over tall skyscrapers. In the bay were lots of boats, and seagulls glided effortlessly in circles.

Mom closed her novel. Dad turned off the radio and quizzed us: "Who knows the name of this famous bridge we're on?"

"It's the Golden Gate Bridge," I replied.

"And do you boys know why this bridge is so famous?" Mom asked.

Buzz and I looked at each other and shrugged.

"This magnificent bridge is an architectural achievement because it was built in 1937, which was a time when our nation was living in the Great Depression and jobs and money were hard to get," Dad said, looking in the rearview mirror.

"As a matter of fact, the Golden Gate was known as the bridge that couldn't be built because of heavy, foggy weather, 100-mile-per-hour winds, and strong ocean currents," Mom added.

"But gritty engineers were determined to succeed and never gave up on their 35-million-dollar dream to build this great bridge, and four years later they triumphed. It's a great story and lesson that I want you boys to always remember. Be determined and never give up on what you're trying to accomplish," Dad said firmly.

Just as Dad finished I thought about my goal. No one was more determined than I was to find that sunken pirate ship treasure and save our farm.

When we reached the end of the Golden Gate Bridge, Dad made his way to the marina where Uncle Milo kept his yacht. Buzz and I gasped when we saw the huge, sleek boats lined up at the dock.

As soon as Dad parked, Buzz and I darted out of the van. With Pugsly following us barking, we raced down the wooden dock. A short distance away I spotted Uncle Milo standing by a large three-decker white yacht that must have been 100 feet long. As we ran up to him, Uncle Milo said, "My favorite nephews. Are you ready for the adventure of your life?"

Buzz and I nodded.

Mom and Dad strolled up, and Mom gave her brother a kiss on the cheek. Dad put his arm around Uncle Milo and smiled. As I looked up, my uncle rubbed my head and messed up my hair.

"I like the name of your boat," Buzz said, pointing to the side of the ship. It read: *Ocean Adventures.*

"And what an adventure we'll have together. This will be the summer you will never forget!" Uncle Milo exclaimed.

Got that right, I thought.

"Come aboard and I'll show you around," Uncle Milo said, leading us onto his boat. As we toured each deck, checking out different rooms, Uncle Milo explained a few basic yacht terms. The *bridge* had the instruments that controlled the vessel's speed and direction; the front of the yacht was the *bow* and the back was the *stern;* the left was *port* and the right was *starboard.* With my new knowledge I felt like a sea-soned sailor.

My favorite place was the entertainment room because it had a pool table, dart board, and a large-screen TV with tons of videos that Buzz and I could watch. Uncle Milo finished the grand tour and led us to his room, where he had a big map of the world. I noticed a red circle marking an island.

"What island is that?" I asked.

"Christmas Island," Uncle Milo said, putting his finger on the spot. "That's where we're going so I can do my research and experiments. It's 1,500 miles south of Hawaii and 119 miles north of the equator. The weather is marvelous year-round, and the water is warm. And if you love fishing, it's a fisherman's delight."

"That's my kind of place!" Buzz cheered.

I found Ticonderoga Island. But discouragement jolted me. It was a long way from Christmas Island.

"Uncle Milo, how far is that island from San Francisco?" I asked, pointing to Ticonderoga.

"Oh . . . five hundred miles."

"Can we go there?" I asked, crossing my fingers on my other hand behind my back.

"If you have a good reason, I don't see why not."

Yes, I cheered to myself. *I don't have a good reason, I've got a great reason!* This was all working out perfectly!

As we were walking out of the room, Mom said, "Now, Milo assure me everything will be okay if you're caught in a wild tropical storm."

"In my thirty years of traveling the sea, there hasn't been a situation I couldn't handle," Uncle Milo said with confidence.

"Relax, honey, the boys will be fine," Dad said.

"Uncle Milo, what are those wild storms like?" I asked.

"Like a roller coaster ride. Up and down, side to

side. Sure does get my blood pumping." Uncle Milo chuckled.

"Cool," Buzz said. I wasn't as thrilled about it as Buzz. I swallowed hard, concerned for the first time about the bad weather we might encounter.

"Boys, get your bags and let's say our good-byes. It's time to shove off," Uncle Milo commanded like a tough skipper.

Buzz and I darted off the boat. Heading down the wooden dock, I slowed down and came to a halt.

"What's wrong?" Buzz asked.

"Oh . . ." I moaned, looking back at the yacht. I didn't know how to put it.

"Bro, what's up?" Buzz said.

"Well—with the talk of wild tropical storms, it's just hitting me that something terrible might happen," I said with a trembling voice.

"Yeah, like what?"

"Buzz, wild tropical storms mean only one thing— a sinking ship."

Buzz shook his head and looked at me like I was some 'fraidy cat.

"Stop freaking out. Uncle Milo's a pro. There isn't a storm out there he can't handle. Now come on," Buzz snapped hitting me in the shoulder.

"Maybe there's one out there he can't conquer. Ever think about that?"

"Know what your problem is? You're wishy-washy. One minute you're gung-ho, the next you're gutless.

Get some backbone, Eric. So what if we're in a wild storm. I'm not scared. We're in safe hands."

Buzz took off down the dock. I stood still frozen. For some reason, I had a bad feeling that in the middle of the Pacific Ocean, doom and peril were waiting for us. *Maybe this is a mistake!* I looked at Uncle Milo's yacht and read the name on the side: *Ocean Adventures.* I took a deep breath. *The name says it all,* I thought looking out at the sea. *Oh boy, there's no turning back now. What am I getting myself into?*

CHAPTER FIVE

Surprises

Our long, long journey officially began as the vessel pulled away from the dock. Standing on the top deck next to Buzz, I waved to Mom, Dad, and Pugsly, who was barking like crazy.

"Good-bye!" Buzz and I shouted, as the yacht picked up speed.

"Be safe, sailors and explorers!" Mom shouted, waving.

In a short time, the marina got smaller and smaller, and soon I couldn't see my parents anymore. Buzz and I held onto the rail, taking in the awesome view of San Francisco and everything else around us. Speedboats were slashing through the choppy waves, seagulls were screeching in the gusty wind, and seals were resting on floating buoys.

This was the first time I had ever been on the ocean. I gazed toward the city, seeing that the once-mammoth Golden Gate Bridge was now a dot. Moments later, the city and the bridge vanished as we were miles into our voyage.

"Good-bye, San Francisco . . . good-bye, Golden Gate Bridge . . . I hope we make it back home," I mumbled with a sigh.

"Knock it off, will you," Buzz snapped, hitting me in the shoulder. "We're not going to die."

"Never know," I replied, looking down into the ocean.

"Whatever . . ." Buzz muttered, shaking his head. He took off as I stood looking down at the ocean. I swallowed hard as fear gripped me. *Way to go, Eric*, I said to myself. *The summer vacation of a lifetime and you're starting the trip with a bad attitude. Some hero you turned out to be. If you don't shake off the fear of the unknown, you won't have any fun, and fun is your middle name.*

After erasing negative thoughts from my brain, I went to the bridge. Buzz was at the wheel steering the yacht. Next to him Uncle Milo was looking at a chart.

"So, Eric, how come you're interested in going to Ticonderoga Island?" Uncle Milo said catching me off guard. Our eyes locked. I knew it wouldn't be smart to blurt out my objective—it would come across as stupid, and I would have to explain the news of our family business being in trouble. It would be like dropping a huge bomb on Uncle Milo and Buzz. My gut told me not to go into it.

Instead, thinking fast I raised my voice four levels, and shouted, "WHO WANTS TO BE A MILLIONAIRE?"

Silence.

"MULTI-MILLIONAIRES!"

More silence.

"What's your point, Eric?" Buzz said, while keeping the wheel steady.

Talking super-duper fast, I rushed into my story of the sunken pirate ship loaded with treasure and how we could become rich. I was talking so fast that I'm sure I set another kid's world record. Uncle Milo kept trying to stop me, but my mouth wouldn't quit. Finally, Uncle Milo covered my mouth with his hand.

"Eric, hold on," Uncle Milo said, "I know that story." My eyebrows shot up. Uncle Milo dropped his hand and said, "Professional divers have been searching for that pirate ship for years. It's one of the great secrets of the sea. Back in the pirate days, pirates would raid other ships and then go to islands and hide their treasure in caves. Sometimes those ships would get trapped in violent tropical storms and sink. Over the years divers have searched for that pirate ship, and it's always been a mystery why no one could discover it near Ticonderoga Island. Two months ago, relentless divers decided to search until they found it—and they did—sixty miles away from that island. Inside they found ten million dollars of gold in a treasure chest." When Uncle Milo was done, I gulped. I couldn't believe what I had just heard. With a quivering jaw I replied, *"For reals?"*

"Yes, I have the newspaper clipping in my library."

My heart sunk like a ship with a huge hole in its side.

"Nice try, bro. Just two months late," Buzz snorted.

Depressed, tears welled up. I bolted out of the bridge onto the deck, tears trickling down my face. I stopped and gripped the cold rail, looking out at the ocean, no land or boats in sight. My head dropped. Project-00 was a failure. My heroic mission was over before it began. The family business was gone. My spirit sunk lower as I watched the boat cut through the waves. A few tears fell into the ocean.

I thought of Mr. Anderson and his dumb coin jar. I slid my hand into my pocket and pulled out the gold coin. It was a dumb coin, and that million-dollar wish was dumb too. Everything was dumb right now. My hopes that my super-secret mission would have worked were gone.

As I was about to fling the coin into the ocean, an arm wrapped around my shoulders. It was Uncle Milo. He looked at the ocean with me for a minute and then said, "Cheer up, sport, you had a kid dream of finding treasure in a pirate ship, but it wasn't meant to happen. The trip isn't over. Maybe you'll find a rare pearl and it will be worth millions."

It was an unbearable loss. I wasn't in the mood to talk; all I wanted to do was sulk. Uncle Milo continued, "If it makes you feel any better, all the years I've studied and researched the ocean, I've never had any luck finding treasure. I'm as unlucky as they come."

I hunched over staring into the ocean. Uncle Milo leaned over the rail. Though he spoke no words, I felt his concern.

All of a sudden we heard a WHOP-WHOP-WHOP booming from the horizon and getting louder. Uncle Milo and I looked up, and I counted twelve, black, super-size, helicopters. As they flew over us the rotating blades rocked my eardrums so that I had to cover my ears.

As we watched the helicopters fly over us, we could see that they were U.S. military and, I couldn't help but wonder *what the military was doing?* We watched them thunder away, and I wished I knew what their mission was and where it was taking them. *What am I thinking? No more wishes for me. Wishing was what got me into trouble in the first place.* I lowered my hands from my ears and looked at Uncle Milo.

"I'm no expert, Eric, but I think the military is training for something big."

"Where?"

"I have no idea."

"Have you ever seen any secret stuff in the ocean?"

"No, but once I was cruising along in the Atlantic Ocean and up popped a huge submarine. Boy, did my heart suddenly race! Over the loud speaker the Navy ordered me to change directions and gave me new coordinates—which I quickly changed to," Uncle Milo chuckled. "I assumed they had a testing zone out there and I was going into it."

A little laugh cracked through my lips as I pictured it.

"I need to go check on Buzz and make sure we're still on course. When you're ready, you're next behind the wheel." Uncle Milo took off, and I was left looking out at the sky thinking about the military. *With all those helicopters, maybe they're making something in the ocean. Hmmm, what could it be?* I wracked my brain, bewildered. Shrugging, I put the coin back in my pocket and went to the galley to get some grub. My stomach was growling, which meant that Mom's pancakes were all gone. I made a peanut butter sandwich, took a hearty bite, and munched away. The only thing on my mind was to save our Christmas tree farm. There had to be something I could do. I was stumped and discouraged. As I was about to give up, I thought, *No way. I'm no quitter!*

I tapped my fingers on the table, drawing only blank ideas. I put down my sandwich, knowing what do to: push-ups. It had worked once; maybe it would work again.

I started fast and, in no time, I was up to a dozen. Just as I was ready to start my thirteenth push-up, something happened. My blood was pumping and the creative juices were flowing. I could feel an idea was trying to come to me, but it was stuck somewhere in the brain. *Come on, you can do it,* I told myself. I could feel it floating around. I racked up another dozen push-ups, and then I stopped. As I rolled over, the idea pulled through and landed with a splat!

Hey, wait a minute. We own a Christmas tree farm, right? I answered my own question by nodding. *And what island are we going to? Christmas Island. And what happens on Christmas? Surprises! There's a strange link. Wait a second . . . how come I didn't see this before?* All of a sudden a tingly feeling went down my spine.

Ohhhhhh, I get it. That's the answer. Christmas . . . surprises . . . they both go together!

There was no way in the world I could guess how my million-dollar wish would come true because it was going to be a surprise! Now that was cool! The more I thought about it, the more excited I became. There was nothing better in the whole wide world than being surprised on Christmas and scoring great stuff. Leaping up, I tossed my arms up in triumph.

"Yes!" I cheered. "That's definitely the answer."

I pulled the coin from my pocket and goose bumps popped up on my arms as I thought about Christmas Island. Squeezing the coin, I had a new attitude, a feeling my trip was now the greatest one on the planet. Everything was working perfectly. My mind raced back to Mr. Anderson and the yard sale; I had this coin and my wish. I had goofed up and made a mistake—I took back everything I had said before, when I had called everything dumb.

Now, for some strange reason it was all coming together. Somehow, some way, my million-dollar wish was going to come true! I felt I had just hit a grand-slam home run! More than ever, I couldn't wait to get to Christmas Island. There would be a great big wonderful surprise waiting for me. The big question was—what would it be?

CHAPTER SIX

Project-OO

At twenty knots, Uncle Milo's yacht glided through the breezy wind and the choppy waves. I stood on the deck. It was strange to see nothing but deep blue water in every direction. Uncle Milo said it would take ten days to travel to Christmas Island; this was our seventh day.

Buzz walked up, and we both inhaled the salty ocean air and felt the wind brushing against our bodies. As we relaxed in the sunshine, Buzz said, "This trip has been a blast. We've seen dolphins, baby whales and sharks—gone swimming and fishing and caught tons of fish."

"Best summer vacation ever—it's only going to keep getting better," I replied. "In a few day we'll be at Christmas Island."

Uncle Milo strolled up and said, "Actually we're making great time. I think we'll be there tomorrow."

I couldn't wait! The tension was building. *What is going to happen?* I wondered.

Uncle Milo went back to the bridge, so Buzz and I

decided to go to the entertainment room. Buzz headed for the television to play video games, and I headed to the computer on Uncle Milo's desk. I decided to use Uncle Milo's satellite link to sign on to the Internet where I typed in *Christmas Island*. In seconds information popped up.

"Hey, Buzz, guess who gave Christmas Island its name?"

"Santa Claus, now don't bug me. I'm busy zooming throughout the galaxy getting ready to assault Alien City."

He's no fun, I thought. The computer screen, blinked, then flickered and I lost my connection. But a second later something else appeared on the screen: **Restricted Area—United States Space and Defense Operations.** It showed a picture of a sleek-looking spaceship zooming around in outer space.

"What happened?" I wondered.

The words *Access Code* appeared on the screen. Just to see what would happen I typed my birthday, thinking the person who programmed the site might have the same birthday as me. After a brief moment, the words *Access Denied* blinked back at me.

I shrugged knowing it would be impossible to get through. *I'm no code breaker, but I'll try one more time,* I said to myself. *This is going to require some clever thought.* I leaned back and put my imagination to work. I was lost, like a bumbling detective you see in the movies, coming up with only wacky codes. Just when I was ready to quit, a sudden thought struck me—I typed *Project-00*, and in seconds a video image appeared.

"WHAT IN THE WORLD!" I shouted.

I shook my head, stunned. I glanced at Buzz, but he was in a state of deep concentration, taking out aliens.

"Buzz, get over here! Check this out!"

Buzz gave an exasperated sigh, "This had better be good, blockhead."

As we gazed at the screen, I gulped hard; the video images on the screen revealed a space shuttle floating on a massive launch platform in the ocean.

"Eric, how'd you do that?" Buzz uttered, staring into the computer screen. "That's your idea—launching a space shuttle from the water!"

"Yeah, I know and I'm completely freaked out about it."

My mouth was wide open in surprise. Buzz did a double-take at me and whipped back to the screen. "How did you find this site?" he asked.

"Got me. I went from the Christmas Island site to this in a blink. This is unreal. This is a military Web site—and they have my idea!"

"They stole it, bro . . . I'd sue," Buzz fired back.

I smirked at Buzz. Together we leaned forward to watch the unbelievable image. The shuttle was in launch position with white steam spewing from three engine boosters. A team of technicians assisted two astronauts in space suits into the shuttle. A short distance away was a massive ship with the name on the side reading *Voyager*.

Then I looked at the site banner across the top bar of my browser. It read *Project-00—a top-secret mission from United States Space and Defense Operations*.

"Project-00! That's *my* secret code name!" I exclaimed without thinking. Not only did the military have the same idea of launching space shuttles from water, but to top it off, they had the code name of my mission.

"What do you mean your secret code name?" Buzz asked.

"Forget it—just something dumb," I said, blowing him off.

I scrolled down the site and saw the different files I could select: *Mission and Purpose, Ocean Location, Intelligence Report, Agency Personnel, Space Defense Weapons,* and *Technology*.

"This is amazing, Eric."

"Got that right."

Scrolling up and down, I opened the *Mission and Purpose* file. It provided incredible information: *Project-00 plays a key role in exploring and conducting top-secret space experiments which will protect the United States from enemy countries.*

"Cool," Buzz snapped, looking at the screen. "Keep going."

We read more files and discovered more amazing information: *Space history was made by launching space shuttles from the ocean to the moon. There a top-secret facility was built where engineers and scientists live and conduct space experiments.*

"Incredible!" I gasped. "Uncle Milo's never going to believe this!"

Flash—another picture popped up and zoomed in on an image of men and women with headsets on seated at computer terminals. Waiting with tension to see what would happen next, I found I had stumbled onto a classified military transmission. Those people had to be engineers inside some mission control room going through pre-launch operations; I remembered learning all about it when I was building my space shuttle in the garage. I'd kept a pile of NASA space shuttle books on the worktable in order to learn how the big boys did their thing.

Another set of images downloaded. Two military helicopters kept circling, capturing full views of the space shuttle on the floating launch platform. The launch pad reminded me of a giant bar of soap as it gently floated in the sea. The surface was flat and its height was ten stories at least. I then caught a glimpse of one chopper hovering, and immediately I recognized it as one of the helicopters that was with the group that had flown over Uncle Milo's boat. *Incredible,* I said to myself. *All those choppers were heading to this secret launch area. Remarkable. . . .*

Somewhere in the ocean this site exists. Where could it possibly be?

"Eric, this is awesome," Buzz said. "They're going to launch that space shuttle from the ocean!"

Buzz leaned closer. I inched my chair forward, too, steadied my eyes on the screen, and pretended I was the launch director and that this was my space shuttle. "Houston, prepare for lift-off. Ten . . . nine . . . eight. . . ." Main engines ignited, and powerful blasts of white smoke shot from the three engine boosters. With wide eyes, I finished my countdown, "Three . . . two . . . one. We're go for launch!"

The engines fired with millions of pounds of thrust, spewing more white smoke as the shuttle thundered toward space. The floating launch platform remained undamaged from the powerful blast-off, but it did cause huge waves to roll across the ocean.

"Wow, awesome!" Buzz and I cheered.

Mesmerized, we watched the thundering shuttle soar toward space. Seconds later, the main boosters released from the space shuttle as it kept soaring higher. The site started to blink, then it vanished. I snapped my fingers to the computer keys, trying to bring it back up, but I failed.

"Keep trying," Buzz instructed as he darted out of the room. "I'm going to get Uncle Milo. He'll never believe this!"

No magic existed in my fingers to pull the site back

up. I leaned back in my chair, stunned at what I had witnessed. *The military had the same idea I did and they actually launch shuttles from the water. Aaamaaazzzing.*

My thoughts were interrupted when Buzz and Uncle Milo charged into the room. Buzz was rambling on about what we had just witnessed on the computer. Uncle Milo snapped his eyes to the screen, but it was still blank.

"You missed the launch of the century!" I gushed out.

"You sure this ocean shuttle launch wasn't some game on the Internet?" Uncle Milo asked, looking at the screen, but it was blank.

"Nope, it was real. Eric cracked into the military's secret site and we saw it blast off. It was awesome!"

"How'd you do it, Eric?"

"Typing letters and numbers into the access code. Bingo, I was in."

"Space shuttles launching from the sea. Incredible!" Uncle Milo exclaimed. He then left the room as Buzz and I stared at the computer screen. The only thing that kept running through my brain was the name of Uncle Milo's boat: *Ocean Adventures.* Slowly nodding, I came to the conclusion that it was the perfect name not only for the boat, but for the trip. *Ocean Adventures*—the name said it all!

CHAPTER SEVEN

Millionaires

I hopped out of bed the following day and looked out the small round cabin window. In the distance I saw Christmas Island.

"We're here!" I exclaimed.

"Cool," Buzz yawned, rolling out of bed.

I raced through getting dressed and flew out of the cabin. I found Uncle Milo on the bridge, holding a mug of hot chocolate and guiding the wheel on the boat with his other hand.

"Big day is finally here, Eric," he smiled at me.

Buzz entered the bridge and we all looked out—we could see the island getting bigger and bigger. I believed that something extraordinary was going to happen to me on Christmas Island. My wish was going to come true!

"Anyone live there?" Buzz asked.

"Small population of people. But we'll be in a remote area, with no one around."

Uncle Milo brought the yacht in and anchored it near the shore. Buzz and I were so excited that when we got to the beach we ran our feet through the pure white sand. It felt clean, like sand that had not been touched by civilization.

The morning passed as we pulled tons of stuff from the boat to set up our camp. I was good at picking names, so I named our campsite *Bare Bones*. We had a big tent, a barbecue grill, stacks of oak firewood, and three ice chests full of soda and tasty snacks.

That afternoon we helped Uncle Milo prepare for his underwater research. The next day he would put on his well-used scuba gear and swim deep into the sea to study ocean vegetation. He claimed that the ocean never sleeps and is alive with an abundance of valuable information which will prove useful for mankind in the years to come.

When dinnertime rolled around, we built a roaring campfire and roasted hot dogs and marshmallows for dessert. As I listened to the popping and crackling wood, I watched the sun slowly set into the ocean. It was so peaceful; it seemed as if angels were gently lowering it down. I rubbed my full stomach and looked around. The island was lush with thick bushes, numerous tall palm trees that swayed in the warm breeze, and gentle waves gliding onto the shore.

I tossed Buzz a thumbs-up. All he did was nod. We both knew, without speaking, that this was like a dream.

That night, the stars covered the sky. We all pulled out our sleeping bags. As the campfire went out, I looked over at Buzz and Uncle Milo. Both had zonked out. I put my hands behind my head and gazed back up at the stars thinking, *This is the summer vacation of my life!* Drifting away, I heard the waves crash on the shore. The last thoughts I remember were, *What will happen tomorrow? Maybe that's the day my surprise will happen . . .*

Early the next morning I smelled bacon and eggs. I don't think I ever missed breakfast my whole life. Buzz was gulping half a gallon of milk from a carton. Uncle Milo handed me a plate of food and we sat around the campfire eating scrambled eggs, bacon, and stacks of pancakes.

"Here's the plan," Uncle Milo said. "I've got a full day of research I need to accomplish so you boys are on your own. Wherever you go hiking make sure you know how to get back to camp."

Buzz and I nodded. Uncle Milo tossed his paper plate into the campfire and left. As soon as Buzz and I had cleared things up and doused the fire, we were ready to do some exploring. We each had a walking stick, a backpack loaded with water, snacks, and a compass.

Wandering deep into the lush green jungle, I kept thinking about my surprise, and that I was on the right trail for my million-dollar wish to come true. *I believe there is a way to get the money needed for our Christmas tree farm*, I thought, *and with each step I am determined to triumph.* Maneuvering past thick bushes we noticed cobwebs with black spiders in the center. A chill went down my spine. As we kept going deeper into the jungle, my mind wandered thinking about headhunters, which triggered a terrible thought. *Islands . . . headhunters. . . . Yikes, what if there's one on the island and it's just our luck to run into him? That's not the kind of surprise I need! Do you know how hard it would be to be creative when your head is missing?* I snickered to myself. Sometimes I could really crack myself up with my wacky thoughts.

Before long we found a canyon with waterfalls and vines hanging from trees. Buzz grabbed hold of a vine and swung to another tree. I saw another thick vine hanging from a tree, climbed up, grabbed hold of it, and announced, "Here I come!" As soon as I pushed off from the tree, the vine snapped, and I crashed to the ground. Buzz laughed uncontrollably.

"Very funny," I moaned, spitting dirt.

I brushed myself off, knowing that jungle swinging wasn't for me. As we left the area, I walked with a slight limp. Buzz was behind me snickering the whole time.

"Should have seen your face," Buzz giggled.

"Pipe down," I grumbled. I was in a lousy mood now and ignored him. After a short time I was thirsty and wanted some water from my backpack. I stopped and turned around. Buzz was gone.

"Buzz," I said, looking around at the jungle. I cupped my hands together and shouted, "BUZZ!"

Nothing.

I was angry at Buzz knowing he was playing a trick on me. I moved through the jungle and kept shouting for him.

Silence.

My heart sank, realizing this might not be a trick.

Becoming frantic, I searched the path back the way we had come—there were no footprints to be found. As I was maneuvering throughout the jungle, I felt a drop of water hit my head. I looked up and dark clouds covered the sky. Within seconds, I was soaked by a tropical downpour.

Searching for cover, I spotted a tree with thick vines hanging down. Dashing in the hard rain, making my way to the vines, I slipped, falling to the ground and rolled down a slope. I came to a stop, wiping mud from my face. The tropical rain continued to pour down, but the rain wasn't hitting me. I had rolled into the mouth of a cave.

I got up, wiped the mud from my hands on my jeans and watched the rain pound the ground. Moments later it stopped and the sun came out. Looking into the jungle, a rainbow formed. My heart accelerated—*that is a good sign!*

I turned around and looked into the cavern. *Maybe he is in here.* Shouting for Buzz, I heard my voice echo. Luckily, I had a flashlight in my backpack.

I'd always wanted to go inside a cave, but not alone. I was too chicken, and besides, bats and caves go together, and I hated bats. I swallowed hard and decided to be brave. If Buzz was in here, he might be in danger, and I needed to save him. I shot a beam of light into the cave and inched my way inside. I encountered jagged rocks and tons of cobwebs as I moved along.

"Buzz . . . are you in here? It's me, Eric," I called out. Silence.

The cave curved back and forth, deeper and deeper, and darker and darker. Soon there wasn't any light from the mouth of the cave. *Oh brother. What have I gotten myself into?* I felt my knees knocking, and that triggered my imagination to take off like a missile. I could visualize a sword sticking out from a skull and a skeleton body with worms and other creepy crawly things hanging off of it. I shook my head, erasing the frightening thoughts.

"Listen, Eric," I gulped, speaking out loud, "just turn around and prove to yourself nothing is there. One, two, three."

I jerked around, flashed my beam of light, and all that I saw was a bunch of cobwebs, minus the spiders. *See, Eric, no skull or bones. Stop freaking out.* My knees stopped shaking and just as I was ready to move my feet, a hand squeezed my shoulder and a deep voice inquired, "What are you doing in my cave?"

Horrified, I shook with terror and screamed at the

top of my lungs. The person behind me was laughing. I jerked around, pointed the flashlight, and discovered it was Buzz.

"YOU JERK!" I shouted, taking a wild swing at him and missing. "I thought something happened to you."

"Nah, I jumped off the trail and found this cave and decided to do some exploring. I knew you would come looking for me."

"Didn't you hear me calling for you?"

"Yep, but I wanted to scare you."

"Figures," I moaned, starting to leave. "Let's go, this place gives me the spooks."

"Hold on, give me your flashlight. I dropped mine and it broke. I want to know what I've been sitting on."

I handed Buzz the flashlight and he pointed a beam of light toward the ground.

"Wow, Eric—check this out!"

I couldn't believe what I saw. Buzz wiped dirt off some kind of chest. Chills went down my spine. *Wow . . . this is my great surprise. The wish. It's coming true!*

"Buzz, open it!" I said with my heart pounding.

He moved the light to the front of the chest. A rusty lock kept the trunk sealed.

"What an awesome find, Eric. Let's get it out of here and open it."

That sounded like a great idea to me. The chest was two feet high and three feet long. It took both of us working together to push, pull, tug, lift, and strain our backs until the chest was finally out of the cave. With sweat dripping, Buzz and I gave each other a high-five.

"I'm dying to know what's inside, Buzz."

"Me, too."

"Maybe someone was hiding it and it's full of money," Buzz said, raising his eyebrows.

"If that's the case, we're in big trouble. It belongs to someone else."

"Ah . . . it's fair game. I say let's take it. Uncle Milo will have tools to get the lock off. Whatever's inside— we split it and I get the most."

"Why do you get the most?"

"Because I put my *rump* on it first and that makes it all mine," Buzz insisted, crossing his arms.

"That's stupid. You're just greedy."

"I'm a business man."

"Whatever."

We worked together, and hours later we got the chest back to our campsite. Uncle Milo was just coming up from the beach and watched us drop the trunk and collapse, out of breath, to the sand.

"We . . . found this . . . in . . . a cave," I said, panting.

"Uncle Milo, can you help us get the lock off?" Buzz uttered, breathing hard.

Uncle Milo took off his scuba gear and circled the chest. He then went to the boat and brought back a hammer. "Well, boys, let's see what kind of luck you have."

With each swing, the tension built inside of me as I wondered what the chest contained and what my surprise was going to be. I was on my knees with my fingers crossed when the lock broke open and fell to the sand.

"Yessssss," I exclaimed, eager to pop the lid.

Buzz slammed both hands on the chest and barked, "Remember, whatever's inside, I get the most."

I flung his hands off and jerked open the chest. Stunned, we all gulped. Hundreds of shiny gold coins! My body shook with excitement as I looked at all that gold. My wish. Somehow it had mysteriously come true!

"THIS IS AWESOME!" Buzz shouted, punching the air.

Awesome is right. This is the greatest surprise in the world! We all dug our hands in and grabbed a handful of coins. Never in my life had I held pure gold. Now I felt the riches of the world in my palms. Each precious yellow coin was smooth and shined in the sun.

"This is the luckiest day of our lives!" Uncle Milo bellowed. "We're rich!"

"How rich?" I burst out.

"Millionaires! Boys, we've got to change plans. Let's get the treasure on board my boat and take off."

"What about your experiments, Uncle Milo?" I asked.

"Forget the experiments, we're homeward bound." Uncle Milo countered.

"Hold on," I said. "Is the treasure ours? People do live on the island."

"Oh, come on, Eric," Buzz groaned. "You think this belongs to someone else?"

"It could," I insisted.

"Fat chance . . . this is ours fair and square," Buzz cried. "What do you think Uncle Milo?"

"Tough call . . . people do live here."

"Guys," Buzz quickly responded. "If someone didn't want us to take it, they would have booby-trapped it with explosives. I'm telling you this treasure is ours."

"I think the right decision is to take it, and there are laws of reporting a find," Uncle Milo said. "We make a claim, and wait. I'm sure we'd be able to keep it and collect our treasure. We will have to pay taxes too, but there would be plenty of money left over. We can divide it and have equal shares."

We all agreed and soon we had our grand prize on the boat with all of our camp stuff. Buzz and I raised our arms and cheered as the yacht picked up speed. As I gazed back at the shrinking island, I could not believe what had happened.

"Good-bye, Christmas Island. I'll never forget you!" I exclaimed.

I left the bridge and walked the deck, feeling great. I was living in a fairytale dream—and it had come true. Mom and Dad would never believe this—I've got the money to save our Christmas tree farm. As we began our long journey home, I felt that somehow that strange coin I got from Mr. Anderson's yard sale was making these things happen around me because of my wish. I reached into my pocket to pull it out. Now, more than ever, I was tempted to spill my guts and tell Buzz and Uncle Milo the news about the family business, but I quickly changed my mind and decided to wait until we were back home and on dry land.

I tumbled the coin in my hand, thinking about what a lucky charm it was. I stopped and gripped the rail. As I watched Christmas Island getting smaller and smaller, a strange feeling came over me. I felt there was something more to this extraordinary adventure, that it wasn't over—it was just beginning. If that was true, I couldn't wait to see what was going to happen next. I was on top of the world! Could any other surprise be as big as this?

Ocean Adventures

Nothing moves as gracefully as a ship on the water. It was our fifth day of the journey back home. As we plowed through the strong wind and the powerful waves, I took up a pen and paper, sat on my bed, legs crossed, and began to write about my incredible adventure.

Homeward bound, our vessel sweeps through the grand Pacific Ocean with ease, with the find of a lifetime. Little did I know that the day I made my million-dollar wish was the day I would start the greatest summer vacation of my life!

Still dazed by the mysterious way my wish was granted, I continue to wonder if there is some magical force in the universe that grants wishes.

As I look forward to my return home, I can say this whole experience, from the time I found the coin until now, has helped me learn a great lesson. Mom was right when she said nothing great will ever happen without determination. For the first time in my life I have maintained good old-fashioned determina-

tion and believed there was a way to get the money to save our family business, and it happened.

To me, determination means to never give up and get up each time you're knocked down. I believe that whatever you want to accomplish, it's within reach by the amount of effort you put into it. I believe that every kid's dreams and hopes can come true—if only they're determined to stick to the task at hand. That's what I believe.

I put my pen down, and looked out the cabin window. The day was bright and not far away, dolphins were swimming together. Of all the creatures in the sea, the dolphin was my favorite. I marveled at their beauty as they moved through the ocean with ease.

Suddenly, I was startled as the door flew open and in plunged Buzz, waving a sword.

"Ahoy there, mate. Look what Uncle Milo found at the bottom of the chest, and guess who gets to keep it? Me!"

I rushed over to Buzz, and examined the three-foot long, double-edged sword Buzz was holding.

"How come you get to keep it?"

"Because I found the chest. Uncle Milo says it's mine by right."

Buzz let me hold the steel sword. I swung it around, feeling like a brave musketeer. Buzz took the sword back and said, "Come on, Uncle Milo has some big news for us."

We entered Uncle Milo's room to find him standing

by the treasure chest with a book in his hand. He was concentrating deeply and mumbled in a faint whisper. Looking up, he snapped the book shut, removed his reading glasses, and announced with excitement, "This is incredible! Boys, I've made a major discovery. You know that we counted a grand total of 9,782 coins. The engraved dates range from 789 to 988, right?" This was true—we had spent the first two days back at sea taking turns carefully counting, stacking, and bagging bundles of 100 coins. Uncle Milo continued and asked, "Do you know what time period that is?"

"Pirates?" I suggested.

"No. Vikings—this is the discovery of the century! These coins are so rare they date back to the Viking age and their value could easily be 20 to 30 million dollars!"

"WOW!" Buzz and I bellowed. A chill went down my spine as I looked at the gold coins. Grinning, Buzz and I gave each other a high-five.

"But I must say, it sure is a mystery how these coins ended up on the Christmas Island; Viking territory was the North Atlantic Ocean."

"Maybe someone later discovered it, hid it, and somehow never was able to come back and get it," I suggested.

"Who cares, it's ours and that's all that matters," Buzz grumbled.

"Buzz is right," Uncle Milo said. "As soon as we get

home, and all of the legal matters are behind us, I'll have the coins and the sword appraised by an expert."

"What does appraised mean?" I inquired.

"To find out how much money they're worth—to the penny."

"Cool. So my sword really was used by a Viking?" Buzz asked.

Uncle Milo nodded. "Vikings were great warriors. A Viking without a sword would be like a kid without sneakers."

Buzz and I laughed.

"What else do you know about Vikings?" I inquired.

"They were great explorers and master craftsmen with exceptional wood carving skills. Not only did Vikings build their ships to be beautiful and fast, they had extraordinary seamanship abilities. They had natural instincts for the sea. Without maps, they could read the ocean and knew what direction to travel and find land. At night, they used the stars and the moon to guide them—and if they did get lost at sea, the challenge to get back on course was never difficult for them."

"All that's good stuff, but forget the history lesson, let's get back to the money," Buzz grumbled.

"It's plain and simple, guys. We're rich!" Uncle Milo exclaimed. "Right now I need to go to the bridge and check on things. You boys stay here and dream about your millions. When I get back I want to hear what you are going to do with all that money."

The news of being mega-millionaires was so thrilling, I felt as if I was floating in the air. *Amazing, I thought. I had a hunch that the adventure wasn't over and I was right!*

"We're rich, bro!" Buzz said, excitedly shaking me.

We were so happy we gave each other a mighty hug.

"What an incredible trip. What a summer this is turning out to be! Not one of our friends will ever believe our story in a million years," I said.

I sat in a chair and started to make a mental list of everything I wanted. At that moment, the boat started to sway, and my thoughts were jolted back to reality. Out the window, I noticed the weather had changed from bright and cheerful to dark and dreadful. I didn't like the sudden change in the weather and wondered if we were heading into a storm.

"Buzz, this isn't cool."

"Big deal, so we're running into a little rough water. Show some backbone."

"This isn't a little rough water. It's a storm isn't it? Storms are a big deal to me. You know how I feel about them."

Buzz put his sword in the chest and moved toward the window. Sighing, he said, "Uncle Milo's an expert at navigating in this kind of weather. Let's go watch a pro battle a storm."

We worked our way up to the bridge. The boat swayed, making us stagger. My gut told me that danger was lurking, and no matter how hard I tried to be courageous, I failed. A feeling of doom was gripping me by the throat. We entered the bridge and I saw Uncle Milo at the helm.

"My radar system shows that we're heading into our first big storm of the trip. It won't take long for things to get pretty wild," he told us.

Buzz and I gazed out at black clouds and huge waves. Thunder shook the sky. Huge drops of rain pounded the sea. The giant waves crashed against the yacht. Lightning bolts streaked across the dark sky. Something was going to happen. Something bad.

"Get your life jackets on!" Uncle Milo barked.

We scrambled toward the cabinet that held the life jackets. This could be the end—no matter how many times I told myself everything would be okay, the feeling wouldn't disappear. I buckled on my life jacket with shaking fingers.

Monstrous waves rolled thirty feet high or higher. The yacht was tossed into the air, and Buzz and I were flung around wildly. Uncle Milo maintained his balance, gripped the wheel, and whipped it around two complete turns to keep the boat facing the waves of the raging sea.

"What are we going to do?" I asked, scared to death.

"Fight this monster, boys!"

"Ever battle a monster storm like this?" Buzz asked with fright in his eyes.

"In my thirty years traveling the sea, I've never fought one like this. Get below, boys!"

We started to obey him, but the ship was tossed violently and we were thrown down, unable to get up or move much. I glanced over at Buzz to see that he had braced himself in the corner holding onto a seat with all his might. I got hold of the one in the opposite corner. Uncle Milo grabbed the radio and barked, "MAYDAY! MAYDAY! COME IN! WE ARE IN BIG TROUBLE! THIS IS. . . ."

Right then, thunder boomed. It was so loud it sounded as if cannons were going off behind us. It startled Uncle Milo so much he dropped the radio. Seconds later, another powerful wave knocked the boat sideways. The fury of waves, wind, and thunder was so terrifying my heart rate accelerated rapidly, and I felt my heart pound my chest.

Just as I reached out to grab hold of Uncle Milo, another wave connected with such force that the boat flipped on its side. Buzz and I lost our grips on the seats as the wheel spun madly out of control.

Then, the unimaginable happened. Water broke the bridge window slamming us hard. I swallowed a mouthful of seawater and grabbed for Uncle Milo, but a second later another mighty burst of water ripped me away from him.

"NOOOOOOOO!" I screamed.

Out into the wild storm I went, tossed by the thrashing, mountainous waves. My lungs burned with pain; this was the end.

"I'M GOING TO DIIIIIIE!" I cried with pure fright.

A piece of wood slammed against me. I grabbed hold of it and hung on for dear life. Another crashing wave took me down into the raging sea. The last thing I could visualize was my mom and dad and Pugsly standing by a Christmas tree. This was it—I would never see them again!

CHAPTER NINE

Hope

My eyes flickered and I coughed. Overhead a seagull screeched. Opening one eye, I saw fluffy white clouds. I opened my other eye to scc two seagulls pass over me.

I'm alive, I thought.

A beam of sunlight shone down on me. I sat up and pain rippled down my back. My head was pounding with a headache and my lungs burned as I released more coughs. Dazed, I discovered that I was on a soft, white sandy beach.

"Where am I?" I mumbled, squinting. I rubbed my head and felt my headache move, splitting me between my eyes. I lowered my head, squeezed my eyes shut, and breathed steadily. I visualized the monstrous storm that had tossed me into the depths of the raging sea. I remembered that one minute I had been drowning, and the next clinging to a piece of wood that kept me afloat, and the next drowning again.

I recalled getting hit on the head with something hard, and then my mind went blank. I had gotten tossed around in the sea and somehow had landed here. *What an incredible miracle that I didn't die . . . remarkable*, I thought, as my headache started to slowly fade away. I got up, took off my life jacket and tossed it down. Looking out at the ocean, tears formed in my eyes. Numerous pieces of wood and debris floated a short distance away. I knew they were from Uncle Milo's yacht. I let out a howling cry, "BUZZ! UNCLE MILO!"

Nothing.

I repeated the call several times, but the only cries I heard were from the screeching seagulls that were circling over me. I looked around with dread. *The storm ripped Uncle Milo's boat apart, and I'm the only one to survive.*

"This can't be real," I moaned, wiping away tears.

I was terrified, thinking I was doomed. I fell to the sand, as more tears rolled down my face. I couldn't believe what had happened. One minute I felt I was king of the world, the next moment that world was shattered and I was stranded on some remote island out in the middle of the Pacific Ocean. There had to be people here—if not, I'd be history!

I turned and saw the island was full of tropical plants and tall palm trees. Farther up on the shore I thought I saw a body. Wiping the tears from my eyes, I looked again, blinked, and realized it was Buzz lying face down in the sand. I leaped up, charged over to him, and cried out, "Buzz! Buzz!"

I rolled him over, tapped his cold, sandy face, and his eyes flickered.

"YES!" I cheered. Buzz was alive!

Coughing heavily, Buzz opened his eyes and said with a raspy voice, "We're alive!"

I pulled off his lifejacket and wiped the sand from his face. He eased up on one elbow, cleared his throat, and said, "Where are we?"

"I've got no idea."

I sat next to Buzz, and we looked out at the ocean. We didn't have to say a word—we both knew our situation was an unbelievable one. Buzz moaned, "That storm . . . everything happened so fast. Uncle Milo, where is he?"

We both got up, and I cupped my hands and shouted, "UNCLE MILO!"

Silence. Nothing. Zippo. Discouraged, I looked at Buzz. I felt we both had the same thoughts: Uncle Milo hadn't survived, and we weren't going to survive either.

"All I want is to be back home with Mom and Dad," I sobbed, turning away from Buzz and looking out at the sea.

"People might be on this island," Buzz said, still rasping.

I wiped away my tears, hoping it was true. Sighing, I felt like somebody reached into my stomach and pulled out my guts. This was the lowest I had ever felt in my whole entire life. A soft wave brought in more wood from Uncle Milo's boat. A backpack washed up on the shore. I picked it up and looked inside.

"Anything good in there?" Buzz grumbled.

I pulled out a flashlight, a Swiss Army knife, and a wet box of matches. I put the knife and matches in my pocket and handed Buzz the flashlight. I then pulled out some peanuts in a plastic bag.

"Wet peanuts. Want these?" I asked.

Buzz nodded his head and I stuffed them in my pocket and kept looking in the backpack.

"Anything else?" Buzz asked.

"Hey, I feel a gun."

"For reals?"

Nodding, I pulled out a black flare gun.

"We've got hope!" I said, excited. "This might save us. Let's fire it up."

"Not yet, let's search around and see if we find people on this island."

"Be a miracle."

I put the backpack over my shoulders. Buzz and I then walked the shore with soggy sneakers. I kept my head down, hoping to see footprints. Nope. I was trying to be positive, but things weren't looking good. As we walked, my thoughts drifted to Uncle Milo. If we were alive, he had to be as well. I stopped and said, "Buzz, I think it's a good idea to fire the flare gun. Maybe Uncle Milo is on this island and he will see it. I'm certain he survived. The ocean is his life, and he's been exposed to the treacherous sea before."

For a long moment Buzz didn't answer. I could tell he was weighing all the choices. Shaking his head, he frowned and said, "Not yet, let's just keep walking and see what happens. If we find him and he's alive, we'll need that flare gun to save us all."

Good decision, I thought.

We walked for a long time and I thought about all those gold coins at the bottom of the ocean. I sighed, knowing they would never be seen again—at least not by me.

"How could this happen to us?" Buzz said, dejectedly.

"I have no idea. And all our mega-millions of gold coins are gone. Poof, history, lost forever. Guess we weren't meant to be rich."

"Guess not." Buzz groaned.

We walked all day and we looked for signs of people. Nothing. The longer we walked, the more depressed I became. My stomach rumbled and I was hungry. I pulled the wet peanuts from my pocket and was ready to munch on them when Buzz nudged me in the shoulder.

"Hey look, bananas!" Buzz exclaimed, pointing toward the edge of the jungle. "I'm starved, let's go for it."

"Sounds good to me."

I stuffed the peanuts back in my pocket and kept up with Buzz as he raced for the bananas. We grabbed ten each from the huge bunches and peeled them like hungry monkeys. They were a little on the green side, but it beat starving.

"Not bad grub," Buzz mumbled with his mouth full.

"What I really could go for is a couple of greasy cheeseburgers and some soggy onion rings," I mumbled back, stuffing my mouth with a banana.

"How about two extra-large cheese pizzas and some chocolate shakes?" Buzz added.

I raised my eyebrows, liking the sound of that. Full of bananas, I slipped the backpack off my shoulders and sat down. "What's going to happen to us, Buzz?"

He slumped down next to me and didn't say a word. He had a stunned, blank look on his face as he stared out at the ocean. "I've always wanted to spend my whole life on a beach, but this is ridiculous."

The waves rolled so peacefully now; they broke on the shore with ease. I reflected on how lucky Buzz and I were to be alive. There was no way in the world we should have survived that violent storm, but we had.

"Buzz, we're alive for a purpose," I said.

"What's that supposed to mean?"

"We should have drowned last night, but we didn't. Somehow, some way, we're alive. That means we're alive for a reason. And I have a feeling Uncle Milo is alive and well, too."

"I hope that feeling is right. So what is the reason for all this?" Buzz asked.

"Got me."

"Well, all I know is that it doesn't get any worse than this."

Buzz was right; it was a frightening situation to be in. I pulled out the matches from my pocket, and struck one. A low flame shot up.

"Buzz, these are waterproof!"

"Cool, let's go get some wood and make a fire. With that Swiss army knife maybe we can catch fish and have some real food for dinner."

That sounded like a great idea. Getting up I put the backpack over my shoulders and we wandered into the jungle. We found all sorts of wood that had fallen from trees and in no time, we had an armful. As we started back to the beach we heard a low hum overhead. It was a WHOP-WHOP-WHOP sound. We looked up and gasped, seeing three black military helicopters. They looked like the same choppers that Uncle Milo and I had seen before.

"Eric, quick, shoot the flare gun! This is our lucky break to get rescued!"

I dropped the wood and the big moment to save our lives had arrived. Just as I put my hand inside the backpack, I heard a twig snap, and my excitement turned to terror. I instantly froze. Ten feet away, eyes were glaring at me from a bush. They weren't human eyes—they were the eyes of an animal ready to attack!

CHAPTER TEN

Top-Secret

"RUNNNNN!" I shouted at the top of my lungs as a German shepherd charged from the bushes. Snarling, it lunged forward, jaws open, revealing its teeth. Buzz tossed the wood he was holding and we both began sprinting through the jungle in terror.

Leaping over fallen trees, darting past bushes and vines, I looked back and saw that Buzz was right behind me, his face white with fear. I whipped my head back around and plunged into a huge, white, stringy cobweb. As it wrapped around our faces, making it impossible to see, I found myself hoping it wasn't poisonous. Just then, we both stumbled, spun around, and went THUMP.

I thought we'd hit a tree, but quickly wiping the cobwebs from my eyes, I saw a man lying on the ground with the wind knocked out of him. Buzz and I frantically looked back, just as the dog leaped at us. Buzz threw his hands on me and we dropped to the sand as the German shepherd flew over us. It landed on top of the man and the animal's jaws snapped down on his leg. He screamed from deep within his gut as the dog tore away at the man's flesh. Shaking, I spotted a rock in the sand, and my reflexes took over. With all my might, I heaved the rock. ZING—it was a perfect strike in the head. The animal released the man and whirled toward me, with blood dripping from its jaws. I froze, shaking from head to toe. This is it! No more running. I was doomed. I covered my eyes. *Good-bye world. . . .*

All of a sudden, I heard another loud THUMP. When I looked, I couldn't believe my incredible luck—the dog had fallen into a pit.

"GO!" Buzz shouted.

The dog barked and growled from the pit as it kept leaping to get out. Lightning quick, we got on each side of the man and lifted him up. He hobbled on one foot, howling with pain, whipping his head back and forth. Making our way through the jungle, we spotted a trickling waterfall. Out of breath, we stopped to rest. The man slumped to the ground, grasped his bloody leg, and continued to moan. His face was incredibly pale, and veins bulged in his neck.

Who is he? I thought. *Maybe he lives on the island.* I examined the jacket he was wearing and realized that I had made a mistake. Over his heart there was a patch that showed a space shuttle blasting off. It read: *United States Space and Defense Operations.* I remembered the top-secret Web site I had stumbled onto. This guy was in the military on some classified mission. That was great news—we'd be saved!

Through clenched teeth, the man cried out for something. I didn't know what he wanted.

"Water . . ." he moaned.

Buzz cupped his hands to get some water from the waterfall, but the man shook his head.

"No," the man demanded. "Water . . . jacket."

I looked at Buzz; he just shrugged. I put my hand inside the guy's jacket, unzipped a pocket and pulled out a canister. The man kept moaning as I snapped it open. Inside was a row of glass vials, each held a clear liquid. I took the cap off of one, and put my hand under his head to give him a taste.

Why does he want this stuff? I thought.

He gulped all the liquid down, and strangely, it relaxed his body. Moments later, however, the man's eyes snapped open. His face flashed red, green, black, and then orange.

I dropped his head and jumped back, shaking. That was the freakiest thing I'd ever seen in my life. *This guy must be an alien or something!* My mind raced. His fingers turned bright blue, then his thumbs flashed pink. Shocked and stunned, Buzz and I stood back with our mouths open.

"HOW DID THAT HAPPEN?" Buzz exclaimed.

We took two more steps back as the man's ears turned purple and his eyes glowed red.

"Buzz, let's get out of here," I murmured.

"Hold on," Buzz said, gripping my arm. "Let's see what else happens. This is cool!"

I wasn't as thrilled as Buzz watching the amazing color show—I was freaked out to the max. The man stopped changing colors and wiped perspiration from his forehead. When he spoke, he did so in short breaths. "My leg . . . the pain . . . it's going . . . gone."

He slowly got up, moved toward the trickling water-fall, and washed his bloody hands and leg. He leaned back against a rock and let the water pour over him. Stepping away, he shook his head like a dog shaking water from its fur. Buzz and I continued to watch, stunned at having witnessed such a bizarre occur-rence. I couldn't believe how this man was free from all that incredible pain. My eyes locked on the man's leg, and I noticed that the blood had stopped oozing. *Whatever that liquid was, it's powerful stuff.*

The man, now clean, came toward us. "That felt like I got zapped by lightning."

"Whatever you say, mister," I mumbled, taking another step backward.

"Hey, I'm not going to hurt you. You saved my life from that ravaging dog. You deserve a medal, kid," the man said, looking at me.

I didn't know what to say. I was scared and stressed out about what I had just seen. It wasn't every day that you saw something so bizarre.

"I don't blame you for being terrified. I'd freak out, too," the man said. "It's not often you watch a person change colors and then watch bone-crushing pain disappear with the swallow of some water. At this point, just keep a cool head and let me explain."

The man moved closer. He was of average height and somewhere in his forties, I guessed. When he took the vial and the canister from my hands, I studied his face. His color was back to normal.

"That German shepherd was hunting me down. I saw guards land on the east shore with dogs and one got away. What they want is me because I have this secret stuff."

"What secret stuff?" Buzz quickly fired back.

The man held up a vial and continued. "See this, boys? This is an experiment from the military, and I was a patient who drank it."

"What is it?" I asked.

"This liquid is moon water. Good old-fashioned, sparkling clean, refreshing water from the moon."

"Huh?" Buzz and I gasped, blown away.

"The military built a secret defense facility on the moon. While on it, a scientist made a major discovery—he found water on the moon. He conducted experiments to find out what effect the moon water had on mice. He tested it on healthy mice, and unhealthy mice, including mice with diseases and cancers, and a major discovery was made. Instantly, the cancerous rodents were healed after the color- changing side effect," the man said, snapping his fingers. "The next step was to test moon water on sick people, and that is when I came into the picture. I volunteered along with two others who had different terminal illnesses to see what would happen when we drank this stuff. When you're on your deathbed with no chance of living, you get desperate. This secret medical experiment was supposed to save us. I was dying of terminal cancer, and it was a miracle when I was cured. But as it turns out, this moon water—it either heals or kills."

"Heals or kills!" I choked.

"Some things it won't cure—some things it will. When I drank it, I got lucky. The others, well, they were unlucky. I was the only survivor, and the military needed to keep me a secret from the world. Little did I know that their plan was to fly me to some secret base and keep me there. I wanted my freedom back. Failing to get it, I took matters into my own hands. What they didn't know was this stuff gave me titan strength. I took out a handful of guards, and I was able to escape and get off the ship they had me on. I got away in a helicopter, and everything was working perfectly until I hit a wild tropical storm. The chopper was hit by lightning, and I crashed on the island. All night I have been on the run, searching for people, hoping they can get me off this island so the military won't capture me."

When he finished his story the only thing I could think was, *What a story. I'm pretty good at making them up—but that one was the best I've ever heard in my life.*

"So let me get this straight," Buzz said. "Moon water can cure sicknesses?"

The man nodded.

"But you had a ravaging dog tear your leg apart. How come blood stopped oozing out from your leg and the pain is instantly gone? How does that figure?"

"Great question, Buzz," I noted.

"Kid, I have no idea. All I know is this stuff is incredible," the man replied. "It's some kind of space wonder cure. I don't know how and I really don't care—it just works. You saw it for yourself, boys; it works."

Silent, Buzz and I thought about that. It was true. What we had witnessed was something out of this world. How? Got me.

"So, mister, you said the military did all this to you," Buzz said.

"Let me clarify," the man said. "The villain isn't the military as a whole. It's one person on that ship who was the mastermind of this experiment. The commander in charge of this mission is the only one rotten to the core and responsible for testing people. In the military, power is everything."

"If he was a dog, what kind of dog would he be?" I asked.

"A pitbull, kid."

"That's mean," Buzz responded, looking at me.

"How do you know so much?" I fired back.

"Be surprised what you discover by snooping around. That's how I got this jacket."

"You said this commander was rotten to the core. Did he tie you up?" Buzz fired back.

"No."

"How about kick you?"

"No!"

"Gagged, blindfolded, perhaps smacked you in the mouth a few times?"

"Kid, you watch too much TV."

"Doesn't sound like that commander was that mean or rotten," Buzz huffed.

"Anyone ever tell you you've got an annoying personality?"

"All the time." Buzz grinned.

I elbowed Buzz in the side to tell him to ease up on the attitude.

"Mister, did you discover any people on the island?" I asked, getting us back on friendly terms.

"The only people I've found on the island are you. What are you kids doing here?"

"We were caught in that same storm and it wiped out our uncle's boat; somehow we ended up on this island without him. All we want is to go home," I said.

"Well, boys, the way I look at it, something's brought us together for some reason."

When he said that, I thought of what I had told Buzz. *There is a purpose to our being alive. Does that have anything to do with him? If so, I am completely baffled.*

"Where's home, boys?"

"Small town in Northern California called San Andreas," I answered.

"How far is that small town from San Francisco?"

"Three hours."

"Hmmmm," the man responded.

I could tell by the look in his eyes that he was thinking. He seemed to be making a plan. I could tell because I acted the same way when the wheels in my brain started spinning.

"So, mister," Buzz said, crossing his arms, "is this whole thing really true?"

With dark, heavy-laden eyes, the man spoke with a sincere voice. "Every word of it, kid."

Buzz and I were silent. I felt in my heart that his story was true. I took one step forward and said, "Mister, my name is Eric; this is my brother, Buzz."

"My name is Adam Joseph," he said, shaking our hands. "Well, boys, there's light at the end of the tunnel, and I'm just the guy who can get you home."

"YES!" Buzz and I cheered, raising our arms in triumph. Just the thought of home made my heart race. We stood, waiting to hear Adam's plan. He cleared his throat and looked deep into my eyes. "Eric," Adam said, "I need your help. If you can help me, I can help you boys."

He then planted the canister of moon water and the vial back in my hands. What in the world was I getting myself into?

Decisions

"You need my help?" I gasped.

Adam took out a small picture from his pocket and handed it to me. It showed a pretty woman with auburn hair. She was standing by a rose garden, her face full of sadness.

"Who's the girl?" Buzz asked, looking over my shoulder.

"A person very special to me who needs that moon water. Her name is Julie Johnson. She has terminal cancer like I did, and that stuff will miraculously cure her too," Adam said with confidence.

Buzz and I looked at Adam with blank faces.

Adam took the picture from me and turned it over. An address was printed on the back. "Here's the address of the cancer home she's at in San Francisco. She's a patient and has cancer spreading in her brain. The chances that the doctors at the Stanford Cancer Center can do anything about it are slim to none. They had taken out as much of the cancer as they could without taking out more of the brain. It's only a matter of time before the cancer will win. Soon she will be gone. The only thing that will save her life is moon water."

By the look in Adam's eyes, I could tell he was determined to help her. He handed me the picture again, and my brain wigged out pretty good. *What are you getting yourself into, Eric? Like you really want to do this. . . . All you want to do is go home and be with your family and forget about this whole trip. It's been nothing but a total disaster.*

Buzz suddenly put his arm around me and said, "Excuse us, mister, I need to talk to my brother."

We stepped away and huddled as if we were in a neighborhood football game. Buzz whispered, "Eric, this is beautiful! Do you see what's happening? This guy doesn't care about the big bucks, but I do. We're in the money!"

"In the money? What are you talking about?"

"Don't you get it? The man said moon water cures cancer. Do you have any idea how much money we could get by selling that stuff when we get back home? Talk about the richest kids in the whole, wide world," Buzz said, beaming. "This is better than finding all those rare Viking coins!"

My heart started to pound like someone trying to break down a door. I couldn't believe it. *The wish—this is how my million-dollar wish is going to come true? This is how I'm going to save our family Christmas tree farm? Through moon water?* I shook my head—it was quite an astonishing moment. I had a good imagination, but this was unimaginable.

I pondered everything Buzz was telling me, got over the shock of such a thought, and focused on the moon water. I saw that Buzz was onto something. If this stuff could cure cancer, like Adam claimed, I could be rich beyond belief—the moon water could easily be worth millions.

"Buzz," I whispered, "what's the game plan?"

"Tell the man you will get the moon water to his friend," Buzz said, eagerly.

Right then, down deep in my heart, I felt like the decision Buzz had made was wrong. More than ever I wanted the money so I could save our farm and be rich, rich, rich. But if we agreed to save the girl, knowing we didn't plan to, it would be dishonest. Not cool. My heart told me it wasn't the right thing to do.

"Buzz," I said with a low voice, "I don't feel good about the plan. If I say we're going to help, then we need to keep our word. That's the right thing to do."

Buzz stared at me like I had six eyeballs. "Are you crazy? We're going to be super rich. I remember when you found that strange coin in that jar. You said that if wishes really did come true, you'd wish for a million bucks! Remember?"

Buzz turned around and the discussion was over. He went back and shook Adam's hand and said, "Okay, mister, we talked it over, and my little brother will go to bat for you. Now, if you don't mind, would you point us to the cavalry so we can be on our way?"

I grabbed Buzz and jerked him away whispering, "I can't believe you said that. What are you doing?"

"Pipe down. From here on out I call the shots." Buzz jerked his arm from me. I sighed and gave up. Emotionally, I was drained from all the highs and lows of this trip. I didn't have the strength to fight Buzz. All I wanted to do was one thing—go home.

"Is that true, Eric? You promise to save my friend?" Adam asked.

I looked straight into Adam's tired eyes. I paused for a moment, nodded and said, "I promise."

A lightning-quick smile raced across his face.

Buzz mumbled out of the side of his mouth, "Good answer, bro."

"Okay, guys, listen up, here's the deal. Helicopters are landing on the east shoreline and military personnel will be scouring every inch of this island to find me. There's no chance I could ever escape. I can hide for a short period of time, but eventually I'll drop and rot to death. My plan is to let them take me in and somehow, someway, escape again. But, you boys, you're scot free and homeward bound." Adam said.

Just the thought of heading home brought tears to my eyes. I could visualize Pugsly wagging his tail and licking my face, happy to see his master. I stuffed the vial and canister of moon water in the backpack and tossed it over my shoulder. I was excited to be saved and the thought of going home made my heart race faster. I looked up at Adam and thought to myself, *Is there anything I can do to help this guy escape from that mean commander? I doubt it. This is a battle he will have to fight and win.*

"So mister," Buzz said. "We have a flair gun in our backpack. Let's shoot it and get the military over here."

"Let's do it," Adam replied. "That will get their attention."

Buzz reached into the backpack, pulled out the flare gun, pointed it to the sky and pulled the trigger. A bright orange flare soared high into the sky and exploded.

"How long will it take before the military moves in?" I asked.

"Not long," Adam replied.

Waiting, looking around at the jungle, minutes passed as we stood in silence. I again looked up at Adam and thought to myself, *So what else is there to this guy's story? Just who is he?* Wanting to know more, I asked, and to my surprise, he grinned. "You boys like action movies?"

"Love 'em," Buzz snapped back.

"You've probably seen my work. In my day, I was one of the top action stuntmen around. I've performed in two hundred movies."

"Cool," Buzz and I said together.

"With my body soaked with gasoline, my body blazing in a special fire suit, I've fallen from burning bridges, towers, and high rises, landing in rivers, lakes, or a huge rubber airbag. The freezing ice-cold rivers and lakes are the worst; you don't get extra pay for those. And since I know how to fly helicopters, I've jumped out of them before they exploded. I've even jumped out of one in a James Bond movie, and landed in a jet boat speeding away at seventy miles an hour—if I missed, I would have been history. I loved the thrill of being tossed out of a New York City skyscraper while being gunned down with fake bullets. I've leaped out of chariots, been bounced off wild horses and bulls, been kicked off trains, hopped off runaway stagecoaches, and hurdled out of countless windows. When it comes to war movies—those were my favorite—I felt like a kid again with fake blood doused over me, and I got to run through the jungle, screaming like a girl."

Buzz and I chuckled. Inside I was thinking, *You're cool. Keep going.*

"Three years ago I called it quits. Broken bones don't heal as fast when you start to push forty."

"Do stuntmen make the bucks?" Buzz asked, eagerly.

"Big bucks. For my last job, a producer paid me two million dollars to ride a surfboard off a two-hundred-foot waterfall."

"Wow, that's what I call riding a wave," I said, impressed by such a feat.

"One hundred thousand gallons of water rush over

the edge of that waterfall every minute. I pulled it off without a scratch," Adam said.

"All I've got to say is, you're one rich dude," Buzz snapped.

"Money isn't everything, kids."

"To a kid it is," Buzz shot back.

Adam smiled, knowing that was true.

"So how did that mean commander find you?" I asked.

"Living in San Francisco, I came down with cancer. I never married and had no family alive to take care of me, so the best decision was to check in to a cancer home. That's where that rotten commander got me. It's all a mystery how I was selected, something that was never revealed to me. But like I said, when you're on your deathbed, you'll take a shot at anything to live."

"So you're a man of action, fearless, a big-time daredevil," Buzz said, raising his eyebrows.

Adam smiled, liking the way Buzz portrayed his character.

The conversation ended as we heard the WHOP-WHOP-WHOP sound of a helicopter. It flew over a mountain and hovered over us. Buzz and I were so excited; we waved our hands as another chopper flew in and together they hovered in the air. Moments later, a military ground unit moved in with radios and guns in their hands. A dozen men swiftly circled us and, on leashes, were German shepherds barking and growling. Adam quickly raised his arms and surrendered.

A muscular sergeant took over the situation. He glared at Adam, and with a deep, commanding voice he declared, "I thought this would be like finding a needle in a haystack. Chain our grand prize and get him back to base."

Slapping thick chains on Adam, they jerked him away. He looked back at me with drooping eyes that made him look like a sad puppy on its way to stay forever in the pound. His face proclaimed what he was thinking: *Please don't let me down, kid.*

A brief moment later, a helicopter descended. They tossed Adam inside and he was gone. I covered my eyes with my hands to block sand that was swirling in the air from the departing helicopter.

"So, what's your story, boys?" the sergeant growled.

I removed my hands from my eyes and answered, "W-we're stranded. A wild storm wiped out our uncle's boat and somehow we ended up here."

"Stranded! Well you're in safe hands now. Is there anyone else with you?" the sergeant barked, tossing a stick of gum into his mouth.

Buzz and I shook our heads.

"Can you help search for our lost uncle?" I asked, anxiously. "We don't know if he's on the island or in the ocean."

The sergeant nodded. "I'll notify air control. We're experts in Search and Rescue missions. If he's out in the sea or on the land, we'll get him. I'll also radio our land unit and have your parents notified that we have you."

I looked at Buzz and flashed him a thumbs-up. He released a small smile. I looked at the sergeant and he said, "What are your names, boys?"

"My name is Eric Thomas, and this is my brother, Buzz."

"Eric, Buzz, did that man tell you anything about what goes on aboard our ship?"

Silence.

We didn't know what to say. We just looked at each other with a blank look. I didn't want to spill my guts and get into any trouble because I knew about the moon water. I was afraid that if I said something they might change their minds and not let me and Buzz go home. I didn't like being in this situation. My muscles tensed.

"Speak up!" the man ordered.

"Uh . . ." Buzz choked. Huge drops of sweat were pouring down his face like he had just taken a shower. I'd seen Buzz nervous when he was in trouble, but never like this—it was unlike him. Buzz started to sway, and then, unexpectedly, his legs buckled and he collapsed.

"Buzz!" I exclaimed.

Alarmed, an officer dropped to his knees to feel Buzz's forehead. "This boy's got a scorching fever," he said.

I dropped down next to Buzz and held his hand. He was out cold.

"Sir, I'm not sure, but this kid could have picked up some type of island virus. His temperature is rising and he needs immediate medical assistance."

The sergeant grabbed a radio from his hip. "Base, be advised we've got trouble down here. I've got two young boys stranded on the island and one of the boys has just collapsed with an extreme fever and is seriously ill. We need medical assistance immediately. Over."

A raspy voice shot back, "The closest emergency room is aboard the ship."

There was a moment of brief silence from the sergeant. Looking down at Buzz, he snarled at his men, "Get these boys aboard a chopper and get them to the ship immediately!"

One of the men took the sergeant aside. "We can't board unauthorized civilians on the ship, sir."

"This is my decision . . . this boy could die! Do it!"

Moving quickly, officers put us on a waiting helicopter. In a blink we were flying over the ocean. Under normal circumstances it would have been totally cool, but with Buzz's life on the line it was terrible. I removed the backpack from my shoulders and thought about reaching into it to give Buzz some moon water. But I remembered what Adam said, that stuff either healed or killed. Too risky. The best thing was to be calm and let the military medical doctors help Buzz.

As we were zooming across the ocean, my breath escaped me. I did a double-take—I couldn't believe what I was seeing! The helicopter was approaching a massive ship. A row of jets sat on the top deck. Not far from the ship on a floating launch platform was a NASA space shuttle with white steam rising from its boosters.

Stunned and in awe, right in front of me, I saw my idea of a space shuttle on a floating launch pad. It was on a grander scale than mine at the school pool and impressive to view. I realized this was the secret military site Buzz and I had seen on the Internet. *Unreal,* I thought. *When I get home nobody will ever believe me. If only I had a camera!*

The floating launch complex was incredible to view from the sky. It looked like a giant bar of white soap floating in the ocean. *What could it be made of to keep it floating?* I wondered. *Perhaps some kind of special rubber?* Whatever it was, just looking at the space shuttle on the launch pad was awesome. On the impressive scale it was a 10! I memorized every detail, not wanting to take my eyes off it. We circled around the launch pad, and my attention shifted to the ship. Ahead of us, the helicopter with Adam aboard landed on the ship's helipad.

I watched guards whisk Adam to an open elevator. The helicopter zoomed off the helipad and our chopper descended.

Waiting for us was a woman in a white medical lab

coat who wheeled Buzz away the minute we landed. I followed as she moved fast and took us down to a medical room. More doctors greeted her and a nurse escorted me into another room. Watching through a dark window in this small room, I saw five doctors work as a team to help Buzz. One doctor moved to a medical tray to put on a pair of rubber gloves. Good thing. Buzz turned his head and ripped one mean, nasty, greenish-yellowish puke where the doctor would have been standing. Nurses scrambled for supplies to clean it up.

The side door to my room opened. My attention shifted to a man with a clean-shaven head wearing a military uniform covered with medals and ribbons. At least six-feet-four, with muscular arms, he moved toward me. I stood at attention, intimidated by his presence and the penetrating glare from his dark eyes. "My name is Commander Evans, and this is my ship," he said with a growl. This was the commander Adam told me and Buzz about—I knew he was the enemy. "If my decision is to let you go, it will be because I grant it, and your future depends on your reply to my questions. Do you understand?"

Swallowing hard, I nodded, knowing I was in deep trouble with my knowledge of the moon water and the experiment. *How am I going to get out of this predicament?* I wondered.

"I expect complete cooperation," Commander Evans said stepping closer to me. "Including a complete account of what that man told you when you encountered him. Now, what exactly did he tell you?"

My knees began to knock. If I failed to cough up the truth, I might not get home. My heart pounded, my eyes flickered, and all I could spit out was, "Ummm . . . well . . . huh. . . ."

Commander Evans poked me in the chest as his temper flared. "Speak, boy!"

I cleared my throat, about to stutter again, when a voice spoke out from Commander Evans' radio on his waist.

"Evans here," he quickly responded, snapping up the radio.

"Your presence is needed in your office, sir. The Director of the Secret Service is on the phone. It's urgent." Commander Evans pressed his lips together and delivered a striking glare at me. "I'll be back, son, and I want my questions answered."

My jaw quivered as I nodded. Commander Evans stormed out of the room and I sighed. *Everything is going so, so wrong.* What had seemed a great idea, being aboard the ship, had gotten me into an ugly situation. It wasn't my fault that I knew about the secret experiment and the moon water. Surely Commander Evans couldn't keep me and Buzz on the ship—or could he? If he did, I would have no choice but to fight back and come up with a plan to save myself and Buzz. Not an easy task for a thirteen-year-old kid from a small town up against a commander trained in combat, intelligence, and warfare. I was definitely the underdog. How could I possibly win?

CHAPTER TWELVE

Big Trouble

Nervous about my future aboard the ship, I paced the room and chewed on my nails. I kept looking through the dark window at Buzz. All I could see was a team of doctors huddled around him.

I noticed another window in the room. Moving toward it, I looked out at the sea. A short distance away, the space shuttle rested on the floating launch platform. *This is so unreal that I came up with something that is used in real life,* I thought, shaking my head. As I focused on the platform, white steam rolled out from the space shuttle's boosters. That meant one thing—launch time. *I've got to see this! Watching a live shuttle launch from the ocean is the chance of a lifetime! I hope I get to see it whenever they launch it.*

My curiosity got the best of me and I decided to check out more of the awesome ship and do some snooping around. I opened the door cautiously, tiptoed out, and went down the hall as silently as a cat burglar. I went into the first door and it was filled with filing cabinets. *I'll bet those are filled with super top-secret stuff,* I said to myself. I tried to open one, but it was locked. I saw a desk nearby and opened the drawer, searching for keys. The only thing I found was a pocket-sized booklet that contained a layout of the ship: Photographs, graphics, and diagrams.

How cool is this? There was a mission control center—a room filled with computers that engineers operated to control all the major systems of the space shuttle. There was also a space research laboratory—a command room in which up-to-the-minute briefings took place prior to lift-off—and a multipurpose room that held racks of clothing, food, and space supplies.

The middle deck had a hospital, a kitchen and dining room area, a library, a fitness center, an entertainment room, and a medical facility. It also had 700 cabins where crew members slept. The bottom deck was a massive vehicle assembly plant. It contained a rocket fuel storage center, a capsule storage chamber, a shuttle booster laboratory, and a shuttle gallery where components were processed.

Hot dang! What a cool souvenir.

I had to take it home to show to my friends, since no one would ever believe I had been on this cool military ship. I shoved the map in my pocket and decided to try different rooms and to keep exploring. I was a kid, and exploring was my middle name. I exited the room and went down the hall and spotted something weird—a red door.

*Why would a door be all red? Must be some classi-
fied stuff in there.*

I had to take a peek, so I opened the door. Entering,
the lights were off and I smelled something very
strange. For a brief moment I wasn't sure what it was,
then I panicked, thinking, *this place smells like
death!* My mind quickly went back in time recalling
a visit I made to the morgue for a school report and
I never forgot the smell!

I shot around to leave, when I heard footsteps coming down the hall. I stepped inside, shut the door, hit
the lights, and in the center of the room I saw a medical table with a long white sheet covering it.

Without hesitation, I dashed under the table. The
sheet formed a tent around my hiding place and
I froze motionless. The door opened and two men
walked in. Their black shoes were inches away from
me. My mouth clamped shut and I remained frozen;
I didn't dare make a peep. They talked as they par-
tially removed the sheet.

"Let's take a look at this guy," a deep voice said.

I gulped hard. *There's a dead body on that table!*
My heart was pounding so hard I thought it was going
to pop out of my body.

"I need to take a blood sample," one doctor said.

I could hear the doctors working on the body.
I imagined a needle going into the arm. Just the
thought of needles makes me shiver.

"So, when does headquarters want this body?"

"Soon."

A limp hand dropped, hanging off the table. My knuckles were white from clenching my hands so tight. Another hand with latex gloves lifted the one that had fallen and placed it back on the table.

"Just to keep you informed, there was an electrical problem in coolers 10 to 24, so I moved all the samples of moon water to coolers 26 to 40."

"How many vials of moon water do we have now?"

"We finished processing the final shipment yesterday, bringing the total to four thousand exactly. Headquarters has a pilot arriving to take all of them today, and since we've got our patient back, he's going to be shipped out too."

Wow, they were talking about Adam. It was scary, yet exciting, hearing all this top-secret stuff.

"This moon water sure is a mystery. Too bad it either heals or kills. Looks like the world will never find out about this, now."

"That's right. And good thing our patient was caught. Can you imagine what would have happened if we had never found him?"

"Too bad he'll never be free for the rest of his life," a serious voice declared.

"What baffles me is when he first came aboard he was so weak—his cancer was so bad that he could hardly stand and lift his head. Then when he drank the moon water he was instantly cured and had the strength of Hercules."

"I'll never forget the colors he went through. Unbelievable."

"It's going to take a team of top scientists to figure out this moon water. You're right, it's a mystery."

"Well, I'm done. I have my blood sample. Let's go."

The two men replaced the sheet and they left the room. I looked at my watch, waited two minutes, and crawled out from under the table. Opening the door ever so slightly, I hustled down the hall, zipping around corners, and made it safely to the medical room without getting caught.

Watching through the window I strained to hear a doctor speaking to a nurse. I was able to hear him say that Buzz had a rare bacterial illness; the next twenty-four hours would be critical. The news frightened me and caused a lump in my throat. Without hesitation, I tapped on the window. "Is my brother going to live?"

The staff ignored me. I kept my eyes on Buzz and he looked seriously ill. For the first time in my life my heart went out to him. Sure, he was a mean brother who liked to tease me all the time, but that's what big brothers did. I didn't want Buzz to die!

He tossed his head, and I could see he was in great pain. He clenched his teeth and arched his back, and the nurses rushed over to hold him down. Fighting against Buzz's motions, a doctor rushed over to stick a needle into Buzz's arm. For a brief moment, Buzz opened his eyes and stared across the room. His eyes met mine and they revealed fear like I'd never before seen in my brother. With all of his strength, Buzz reached out toward me. Then his eyes closed and his body went limp. Whatever that doctor had shot into Buzz had immediately knocked him out.

The medical staff moved into another room and closed the door. I slumped in a chair, determined to do something. *Enough is enough,* I thought. I made up my mind to take matters into my own hands to save Buzz. My plan was dangerous, but I had to help my brother. He needed to drink the moon water, and I knew that it could cure him. Sure the stakes were high, but I had to do something—I couldn't bear to see him in so much fear and pain.

I looked around for my backpack.

"Oh no! The backpack is gone!" I choked. "Where is it?"

I scanned the room—it was nowhere. It wasn't in the room where Buzz was lying helpless either. *How could this have happened? Think,* I told myself. *Where could it be?* Oh no, somehow I must have left it on the helicopter. It was the only place it could be. I'd been so wrapped up with Buzz and this incredible ship that I had forgotten to take the backpack with me when I rushed off the helicopter.

Cold sweat rolled down my forehead. I was in huge trouble. If they looked inside, they'd find the canister of moon water. *How will I explain that? Don't panic, Eric. Keep a cool head,* I kept telling myself.

I took several deep breaths, pulled myself together, and put first things first. It was time to take care of business and help Buzz. I looked at the ship map and tried to figure out in what room the doctors would keep the moon water. I found a room marked cold storage. This had to be the place where they kept the moon water, because I recalled a doctor speaking about an electrical problem in the coolers.

Firm with my decision, I moved out of the room in pursuit to swipe some moon water to save Buzz. I used the map and moved swiftly down the halls and found the room I wanted, but I had a huge obstacle in my way. A guard was sitting in a chair and next to him was a German shepherd.

That's one tightly guarded room, I thought. *How am I going to get in?*

Hiding behind the corner, scratching my head, thinking of a way, I heard the guard speak into his radio, "Base, it's break time. Do you have someone nearby to take over my watch? Over."

"Relief will be there in one minute. Go ahead and take off and take lunch. Over."

I carefully eased around the corner and watched the guard leave the guard dog and walk down the hall. That was my lucky break. One down, one to go. *How am I going to get past that guard dog?* I remembered I had some wet peanuts in my pocket. I pulled them out and flung them down the hall. The dog went after them and I raced for the door and made it inside.

"Yes!" I exclaimed, closing the door. I had one minute to work fast!

The room had rows of coolers and I knew instantly this was the place they kept the goods. Stepping over to them, I put my hand on a silver handle, jerked it open, and my eyes flew open gazing at a dead body! My face was inches from a cold white foot with a numbered tag tied around the big toe.

"AAAAAAAAH!" I screamed, slamming the door. *That's the other one who didn't make it, like Adam told us.* I closed my eyes and pulled myself together. When I had finally calmed down enough to open my eyes again, I saw that I had opened door Number 5. I scanned the numbers on the other coolers and found Number 26, which I remembered the doctor said was where he transferred some of the moon water. I popped it open and cool frost floated out in waves. Waving my hand, wiping away the frost, I grabbed two ice-cold vials. On the side of the vials, printed in black lettering, were the words: MOON WATER.

I stuffed them in my hip pocket and darted for the door. Slightly opening it, I saw the guard dog. Growling, it revealed its teeth. I tossed the last wet peanut on the floor inside the room. The dog entered the room going for it. I slammed the door and wiped sweat from my forehead.

While running down the hall, turning corners, hustling my way back to Buzz, I came to a halt when I saw two doctors coming out of a room.

"Hey, kid, what are you doing?" one of them barked.

Alarmed, I looked left, then right, then ran like a scared mouse. They charged after me, and I panicked. I had no idea what to do so I took off running and got away from them. As I zipped around another corner, I quickly discovered it was a dead end. I leaned against a closed door shaking with fright.

Unexpectedly, the door I was leaning against opened, and I fell into a dimly lit room. I kicked the door shut and fumbled around, discovering something that felt like a barrel. I had no choice, so I opened it and jumped in. What a terrible thing that was! Every one of my muscles was tight with fear. I tried not to make a piercing scream as I felt furry, creepy, crawly things with tiny claws move up my leg, down my shirt, and onto my head. I deserved the highest medal for bravery that a kid can get for not letting out a peep. At that moment I heard the doctors charge into the room and light was shining through the rim of the barrel.

"I thought he went in here," a deep voice insisted.

"The barrel," said another voice.

"No Mel, the kid wouldn't jump in there. See what the sign says? LAB MICE—DO NOT OPEN. TEST ONLY."

"Yeah but. . . ."

"Mel, drop it. The kid's someplace else. Somehow he got by us. Commander Evans was right. Those kids are nothing but trouble."

The door shut and I bolted out of the barrel with mice all over me. I shook my pants and shirt, sending white lab mice zipping across the floor. Chills went down my spine. Everything I was doing was turning into a nightmare. What else could possibly go wrong?

CHAPTER THIRTEEN

Danger

How could I get back to Buzz without being captured? I didn't want a repeat performance of running away from anyone. Luckily, I had gotten away—next time, my luck might change.

I noticed a vent high up on a wall. A cool smile rolled across my face. I whipped out the ship booklet, flipped to the map, ran my fingers over a possible route through the ship's ventilation system. I could crawl my way back to Buzz. It was worth a try; I pulled the Swiss army knife from my back pocket, then pushed a chair under the vent. I stretched on my tiptoes. Just slightly short of reaching the screws with the knife, I exerted extra effort. My toes ached. For the first time in my life I was standing on my toenails. Determined, I managed to get the knife's blade into a screw and used it as if it was a screwdriver. Turning it delicately with my fingers, I successfully unscrewed the screws from the vent.

"Yes," I sighed, victoriously pulling the vent cover from the wall.

I struggled to pull myself up and crawled inside. It was tight, but on my knees I was able to move forward. I hoped there were no rats inside the ventilation system—the lab mice experience had been enough for me!

As I moved toward another vent, I heard voices. I slowed down knowing from the map what room I was coming up to. Inching my way forward, barely breathing, I peered down through a dusty vent. I knew I needed to be extra careful—sniffing all that dust could make me sneeze and blow my cover.

The room was filled with five officers seated at a long table. At the head of the table was Commander Evans. He was restless, tapping his fingers on the table. I strained my ears and listened to what he was telling them.

"As senior officers, the following remains a need-to-know classified fact. Disclose it to any party and you will be subject to military action. Don't argue and don't question. Just follow orders," Commander Evans snapped.

The officers responded to Commander Evans' powerful voice and, in unison, they nodded. A senior officer stepped forward and proceeded to pull my backpack from a green trash bag. I kept my eyes fixed on my backpack, knowing I was about to get into deeper trouble than I was already in. The officer pulled out the canister of vials and placed it on the conference table. My stomach twisted into knots.

"This was discovered in the helicopter that the boys were in, Sir," the officer announced.

Commander Evans leaned over the table. "Moon water has mysteriously jumped from our medical facility into a boy's backpack?"

The officer continued. "Yes, Sir. And the news unfortunately doesn't get any better. The younger brother, named Eric, is missing and we haven't located him."

Oh great—I'm in big trouble! If only Buzz had been okay, he could do all the talking. He was an expert at talking his way out of anything.

Commander Evans pounded his fist on the table and barked, "Because of this, our security has been compromised. It's obvious the patient stole moon water from our medical facility, and when he was on the island he gave it to the boys and told them about the secret experiment. That's a huge problem. Only the highest levels in Washington knew we were testing the terminally ill patients and the President hasn't been informed yet. Headquarters didn't want to inform him that moon water was tested on humans until we knew more about this phenomenon. It was a mistake, a blown mission. What has happened needs to be quietly swept under the rug, as if this never happened. We did not expect two deaths from drinking moon water. At this point, we must silence all threats of exposing this experiment. The boys will not be going home. Sergeant Olsen, cancel the search and rescue for the boys' uncle immediately and do not contact the boys' parents."

We're not going home! What will they do with us? I was so scared, my jaw started to quiver. One of the guards asked, "Sir, may I clarify a point? We're not letting the boys go?"

"Let me tell you something, and don't you forget it," Commander Evans snapped. "Kids talk and that's the last thing we need. The world can't find out about this moon water and the experiment and what has happened. If any unauthorized person gets off this ship, our security will be breached. I want a military manhunt to find that missing boy. Once you do, get rid of him and the other boy as well. And I don't care how dirty the job is, either."

Those cold, harsh words hit me like a rock-solid snowball. I couldn't believe what that ruthless commander had said. My heart was pounding so hard now that I thought someone might hear it and discover me. I put my hand into my pocket, grabbed my coin, and pulled it out. I wished I could make one more wish to get us out of this situation. I couldn't imagine how we would get off this ship.

Commander Evans' jaw muscles were tight as he stood. "Now, listen up, men," he barked. "We're in a tight spot. A short time ago I spoke with the Director of the Secret Service and he informed me that one hundred agents will arrive today because the President and Vice President want to see the next shuttle launch firsthand. They are scheduled to arrive at twenty-two hundred hours, stay onboard, and witness in the morning all aspects of marine operations and procedures leading up to the launch at zero seven hundred hours. All ship personnel on decks Two and Three will relocate to decks One and Four. Those orders come directly from the Director of the Secret Service. Prior to our meeting, I spoke to senior officials at headquarters and they want all the moon water, the living and the dead experimental subjects off the ship because the Secret Service will comb it from stem to stern."

The room was silent. All eyes were on Commander Evans as he continued. "A chopper is en route and will land at fifteen hundred hours. At sixteen hundred hours the Secret Service is scheduled to arrive, which puts pressure on us to load the secret cargo and quickly get it off the ship. Right now we need a plan. Headquarters' helicopter will arrive shortly and I don't need a situation to arise. Should the Secret Service get here before Headquarters leaves, we've got trouble. How would we get the patient off the ship under their lurking eyes?"

A muscular officer with a thick neck raised his hand. "Sir, I'm an expert at force, and I'll personally make sure he's sleeping like a baby, in a box, and the Secret Service will never know when we load him onto the chopper."

Commander Evans nodded. "Good, that's the kind

of aggressive action I like. Now, where are you holding the patient?" he asked.

"Sir, he's chained to a steel pole in the mechanical room. He's not going anywhere," an officer answered.

"Excellent. I'm going to interrogate him. He's going to pay for escaping from my ship with the moon water and giving it to those kids."

As soon as Commander Evans said his last word, he left the room.

"Okay, guys," an officer said, lowering his voice. "I've got an idea of how we can get rid of the boys. Listen up, here's the plan. . . ."

As much as I strained my ears, I couldn't hear what he said after that. It was a soft mumble and I couldn't make out one single word. It was time for me to flee the scene—things were getting out of control.

I put the coin in my pocket and crawled fast, zipping around corners, trying to get to Buzz, knowing our lives were in danger. I passed several vents, peering through each one, looking for Buzz. Nothing. Full speed ahead I charged, as my thoughts raced between finding Buzz and, somehow, some way escaping off this ship. *How? I have no idea,* I said to myself. Turning another corner, near another vent, to my surprise I came upon Adam chained to a steel bar, just as I had overheard.

Commander Evans' voice barked over the guard's radio. "Guard, don't take your eyes off our man. Remember, he has remarkable strength."

"Everything's under control down here, Sir," the guard replied, chuckling in Adam's face. "He's not going anywhere on my watch." The guard then took a seat at a desk, kicked his heels up, and looked at a covered plate. He chuckled, taunting Adam. "Mmm, I get dinner, you get nothing." The guard licked his lips and removed the silver lid from the platter. On top of his food sat a mouse.

"AAAAAAAAH!" he shouted, leaping to his feet.

The mouse was eating an olive from the plate and scampered to the floor, zipping past the guard, darting under a desk. The guard grabbed a broom and rushed after it.

While the guard was scrambling around, poking the broom at the mouse, Adam's eyes turned mad-yellow, and the veins in his neck rippled. He flexed his arms and expanded his chest like a world-champion bodybuilder. Breathless, I watched his arms bulge to the point that he looked like a muscular character from the cover of a superhero comic book. The chains snapped, crashing to the floor. I was so shocked I could hardly breathe witnessing Adam's brute strength; all because of that mysterious moon water—amazing!

Then I saw the mouse as it scampered out from the desk between the guard's feet. "I'll show you who's boss!" the guard sneered. He raised the broom over his head and spun around, ready to swat the mouse, but was taken by surprise when Adam greeted him with a punch to the chin. The guard's head snapped back, the broom fell out of his hands, and he dropped backward, out cold.

Adam saw the mouse eating the olive and said with a quick smile, before vanishing from the room, "Thanks a lot, little fella . . . I owe you one."

"Hey!" I yelled shaking the vent. Too late, Adam was gone. He was on the run, looking for a way to escape off this ship, just as I was. As soon as I found Buzz, I wanted to find Adam. He successfully got off the ship once—I knew he had the brains to do it again and I wanted to make sure Buzz and I were with him.

My thoughts went blank when Commander Evans stormed into the room and choked seeing the guard knocked out on the floor. I watched him snap the hand-held radio from his belt and scream into it, "SECURITY—THIS IS A CODE RED! THE PATIENT HAS ESCAPED!" His face was red with rage. He slammed the door as he charged out of the room.

I put my head down and crawled full speed ahead. My life was on the line. I couldn't believe a person could be so ruthless as to want to end Buzz's life and mine. It was time to start wracking my brain, to put a plan in motion to save us. What did I have to my advantage? I slowed down knowing I had the perfect super secret weapon up my sleeve—my ingenuity. It had never let me down!

CHAPTER FOURTEEN

Fighting Back

As I moved swiftly again through the dark crawl space my knees throbbed with pain. *How much longer will I have to keep crawling?* I wondered. I felt as if I couldn't go one more inch. I clenched my teeth, blocked out the pain, and hoped that I might soon find the medical room. The way had looked so simple on the map, but getting there was turning into a nightmare.

I heard moaning sounds. With my last burst of strength, I struggled to the next vent and gazed down. The medical room at last! Buzz was on his last breath, sucking air hard.

Buzz groaned, tossing his head back and forth. His shirt was soaked with perspiration and his face was grayish looking. It appeared the medical team had left Buzz alone to die. So that was the plan for him. But me? Couldn't think about that now.

Furious, I kicked the vent open, slid out, and rushed over to Buzz. I pulled the vial from my pocket, popped the cap, and with a trembling hand, put the vial to his mouth. Luckily, Buzz swallowed the moon water like a dog that hadn't had a drink in days. I was shaking, hoping I was doing the right thing. Doubts entered my mind. *What if I kill him? How will I live with that? If I lose Buzz, there's no one to blame but me. It will be all my fault—the worst thing to ever happen!*

Buzz gagged, spit, and choked. He bolted upright and went into a harsh coughing attack. He hacked so hard slimy balls of green stuff flew out of his mouth. Hearing Buzz gag and wheeze made me panic. *I made the wrong decision—Buzz is going to die!*

His eyes popped open and he grabbed me by the collar.

"HELP—I can't breathe!" he gasped.

I didn't know what to do. Suddenly, Buzz's eyes flashed red, then black, and finally green. His nose turned bright pink. His left ear turned blue, then orange. I gulped hard witnessing such a strange sight. Shaking my head, I was stunned at the side effects moon water had on people.

Buzz let go of my collar as the colors started to fade. His breathing settled to a normal rate as he inhaled and exhaled, then took several deep breaths. With a raspy voice he stammered, "E-Eric, you ss-saved me."

I couldn't believe it! It worked! I blinked a few times to come out of my daze. I helped Buzz to his feet. He rolled his neck and shook his arms. "How'd you do it, Eric?"

"Moon water!" I said, excitedly showing Buzz the empty vial.

"What?"

Terror rattled Buzz so hard that he grabbed my shirt. Shaking me, he roared, "You could have killed me, you numskull!"

"It was the only thing I could do to save you," I said.

Tossing me aside, Buzz's full attention went to a small mirror on a wall. He checked out his face and mumbled, "I look the same—right?"

"Listen to me, Buzz. We've got to get out of here before we're dead meat."

"Dead meat! Where are we?"

"We're on a top-secret military ship. This is the ship that Adam told us about, and I've overheard the commander say he wants to get rid of us because they found my backpack on the helicopter with the canister of moon water inside of it. Buzz, we should have never found out about that stuff. The commander ordered officers to get rid of us because we know too much!"

Buzz's face registered both shock and stress. I didn't blame him for one minute.

"Why is it such a nightmare to get home?" Buzz asked.

"I don't know, but I'm determined to get us free."

"Oh yeah, how?"

"By using my brains. Now let's get out of here before someone comes in."

We charged for the door and I had barely touched

the handle when I heard a low static sound coming from somewhere in the room. We followed the sound to a cabinet. Inside was a black mobile military radio. My mind flashed back to when Buzz and I were little—we used to pretend we were in the army and used walkie-talkies to talk back and forth at the imaginary battlefront. Dad got them for us at a yard sale, cheap plastic toys. But this radio—it was the real thing. I pulled it from the cabinet; it was heavy and had all sorts of channels. Through the static, Buzz and I could hear a deep, harsh voice.

"Hard to call foul play without bodies," a voice said.

My ears shot up like antennas.

"Can you believe they're going to get rid of those kids the dirty way?"

Buzz kept shaking his head.

"How are they going to do it?" a younger voice asked.

"The plan is to. . . ."

Right then, the radio went dead. "Oh, no! That's not a good sign. Buzz, we've got to get out of here! I've got a ship map. Follow my lead."

I snatched the ship map from my pocket and looked for the room I wanted.

"Hey, Eric," Buzz said, hitting me in the side.

"Adam said moon water gave him titan strength. Let's see what happens to me."

"That's right," I said eagerly. "An excellent secret weapon the enemy won't expect from a kid."

Buzz moved into a catcher's position next to a filing cabinet. With both hands underneath, he jerked, pulled and grunted. The cabinet didn't budge. His face turned beet red. Why did Buzz lack the superhuman strength Adam had? This moon water stuff was some seriously twisted liquid. I doubted anyone on this planet would ever figure it out.

"Forget it, Buzz. That stuff backfired on you."

"Hold on . . . I'm almost there . . . It hasn't kicked in yet. . . ."

Buzz continued to grunt and moan. Finally, with all his strength gone, he gave up. Out of breath, he got up, annoyed at not having titan strength. "You sure you gave me enough?"

"Enough to make you better," I fired back.

Looking at my watch, every second was crucial. No time for useless talk, we had to hurry. "Let's go," I said. We scurried out of the medical room, crept along halls and up and down the deserted decks. It was kind of like being home, sneaking around the basement or the attic, pretending we were in danger; the thing was, this time it was real.

Buzz came to a sudden halt when he passed by a window and saw the space shuttle on the floating launch pad. He did what I did when I saw it, too; a double take, not believing his eyes.

"What in the world? That's your idea, bro. Awesome."

Hearing voices coming down the hall, I jerked Buzz

by the arm as he continued to gaze at the shuttle on the launch pad. As we flew around a corner, we caught a glimpse of a guard with a German shepherd on a leash.

"Oh, no," I moaned looking at Buzz. "They're using dogs to hunt us down."

Fast, yet quietly, we motored down the hall and flew into a nearby room to get away from the guard. The room was pitch-black, but I knew where we were the second we entered, the laundry room—I could smell the soap. We scrambled in the dark, bumping into a wall, and stumbled into a huge, round, deep, tub of clothing. Crawling in, we dug to get to the bottom and didn't make any noise.

The door opened, a light came on, and we heard footsteps. My hands trembled with fear that we could get caught. A radio crackled. "Be advised, I'm in the laundry room and so far nothing. Over."

A clear voice responded back, "Keep searching, those kids are somewhere on this ship. Over."

The footsteps moved then stopped, and doors opened and closed. The footsteps continued on and moments later I could hear the dog sniffing. He let out a bark and scratched the tub. "Smell something, boy?" the guard said.

Busted! I moaned to myself.

The lid opened and the guard groaned. "This stuff reeks! You smell nothing but terrible body odor. These clothes need to get washed ten times to get the nasty smell out. Glad laundry isn't my department." He then closed the lid.

"Be advised, laundry room all secure. Over."

"Maintain your pursuit. Over."

"Ten-four."

I heard footsteps exit the room, and the door close. I raised my head up and saw that the lights were still on.

"Buzz, the coast is clear," I whispered, tossing off the dirty clothes.

Buzz shot up with a stinky pair of underwear wrapped around his head.

"Oh, for crying out loud!" Buzz moaned, pulling off the underwear and tossing it aside. "I'm ready to puke."

"Shh! That was close, come on," I whispered.

We crawled out and I saw tons of powered laundry soap in big tubs.

"Buzz," I said with a grin. "I've got a sneaky plan up my sleeve. It's payback time. Time for some revenge," I said, raising my eyebrows up and down.

"What are you thinking, bro?"

"I'm going to hit 'em where it hurts. Grab an empty bucket and scoop up detergent until it's full."

"Need to clean your underwear, sport?" Buzz cracked.

"Be quiet, Buzz, I've got a dirty trick. It will really mess them up."

"What's the plan?"

"You'll see," I snickered.

"Eric, you know I'm the king of rotten, and a mischievous plan is right up my alley," Buzz protested.

"I've got a winner idea that will really screw up their next launch," I said, with a mischievous smile.

With the aid of the ship map, we darted out the laundry room without spilling anything out of the bucket. Skillfully navigating our way to the next location, we quietly crept into another pitch-black room. Unsuccessful at finding a light switch, I reached into my pocket, pulled out the water proof matches that I had saved from the backpack, and struck one. We used the flame's glow to look around the room. Our eyes sprang wide open on reading the big, dark, bold words printed on a tank: **FLAMMABLE ROCKET FUEL.** "EEEEEKKKKKK!" Buzz shrieked, blowing out the flame. "We're in the rocket fuel room!"

"Hot dang, perfect navigating, if I do say so myself," I exclaimed, striking another match.

"What are you doing? Trying to launch us to the moon?"

"Pipe down, Buzz. This is my revenge plan."

I put my bucket of soap down, found a light switch and flipped it on. With the aid of a nearby ladder, I made my way onto the silver fuel tank. I tried to get the lid open, but it was locked.

"Check for keys," I whispered. "The lid won't budge."

Reluctantly, Buzz fumbled through a desk drawer and found a set of keys. "Here, see if these work," Buzz said, flinging them up to me.

Trying each one, I found the one that fit.

"Hand me the bucket," I said.

Buzz heaved it up to me. Opening the tank, I poured all the detergent into the tank and then locked it again. I jumped down and put the bucket in a storage bin which had racks of work suits for the fuel engineers.

"Now what, Eric?"

Turning to Buzz with a big grin, I said. "I'm not a scientist, but shuttle fuel and laundry detergent don't mix. Detergent in the fuel lines will really screw up their next launch. This is my way of sending a heads-up message to Commander Evans: He's messing with the wrong kids. We're fighters. Next launch, the shuttle will have so many bubbles spewing from the engine it will be bubble city."

"Very, very funny, genius. Nice to see you can find humor when our lives are on the line. What you should be thinking about is getting us free. I want to go home!"

"Don't worry. I've got an idea that just might work. Listen up, this is what we're going to do. . . ."

Escape

Little did I know that being a whiz with computers, electronics, and gadgets might someday save my life. With strategic planning, my idea could work. As I studied the ship map, it was clear that the mission control room, where they supervised the launching of the space shuttle, was the place we needed to get to.

"Eric," Buzz rattled, "what's the plan?"

"I have to get inside the mission control room," I replied. "It's jam-packed with high-tech computers, radios, and satellite capabilities. All I need is a little time, because of the satellite links. I think I can make contact with TV stations worldwide and spill my guts. That media attention will spin all over the world and go straight to the White House. While I was sneaking around, I heard the commander tell the guards the President and Vice President are coming on board at ten o'clock tonight, and wherever he goes, so does the Secret Service. They arrive at four o'clock to secure the ship. If my plan works, they will investigate immediately, and we will be saved! And going home!"

"The President and Vice President are going to be on this ship!" Buzz said amazed. Then grumbled, "Hold on, if you know the Secret Service will be here, why not hide and let them find us?"

"Because the enemy might find us first before the Secret Service does. Trust me, Buzz, we've got to stay on our toes, thinking of ways that will help the Secret Service to immediately move in and investigate."

"Fine. So how are you going to get into the mission control room?"

"That's where you come in," I said, grinning.

"Me?" Buzz shook his head.

"All ships have alarms, and we need them to go off. That's how we can get those mission control engineers out of there so I can move in."

"And how am I going to do that, genius?"

"By working your way to here," I said, pointing to the ship map.

Buzz looked down and gulped. "The weapons room!"

"Bingo. There's got to be something you can do to make an explosion so the alarms fire."

Buzz's eyes lit up and a devious smile eased across his face. I could tell he liked the word *explosion*. Every Fourth of July, Buzz was the king of fireworks, a real enthusiast of fire, smoke, and objects that lit up the dark sky with red, white, and blue sparks. His most prized creation was a bunch of sparklers attached to a bottle rocket—he would launch it 75 feet into the air and watch it whistle, pop, and explode, shooting out bright colors in all directions.

"Here's the deal," I said. "Once inside the weapons room you're in fireworks city. When the alarms are blaring and chaos sets in, we make our way to the mission control room so I can do my thing. From there, we'll use this map and find a safe place to hide."

"Too wacky . . ." Buzz grumbled. "I don't have a good feeling about this."

"Give me some credit. I'm trying to do something to save us."

We took off down the hall and two guards were coming out of a room. Buzz grabbed me by the shirt and we darted into a nearby room. It was pitch-black and we again fumbled around. Minutes later, the guards entered and turned the lights on. A safe distance away from the enemy, hiding under a table, I couldn't believe where I was and what I saw—a row of space shuttles on one side of a huge assembly hall. I sat stone still, every sense on high alert. Cautiously, I whipped my head around, looking left and right for Buzz—he was gone.

Oh, no—what do I do now? Where is he? I wondered. Panic raced through me. . . . "Psst . . . Buzz, where are you?" I whispered, sharply.

Silence.

I took a deep breath, trying to think, trying to stay calm. Suddenly, I felt the urge to sneeze. *Bad timing,* I opened my eyes wide. I wiggled my nose. I tried to fight it off—but I lost the battle.

"AAAACCCCCHHHOOO!" I roared; it was from all that laundry soap. The sneeze echoed in the assembly hall as if it was the Grand Canyon.

"Over there!" a deep voice ordered.

Footsteps came charging toward me. I zipped away from the enemy, who was gaining on me. This was it. This was the end. I was a scared mouse, trapped.

As I darted past one of the space shuttles a door shot open. I was about to run past it, when Adam leaned out and grabbed me and pulled me inside.

He held me tightly as he closed the door and locked it. I looked around for Buzz, but he was nowhere to be found. Adam's eyes met mine. We remained motionless and listened intently, waiting. Moments later, the door handle jerked. It jerked again, harder.

"We're doomed!" I choked.

"Not with me around, kid," Adam fired back through gritted teeth.

Adam snapped the door open throwing the guards off balance. He jumped toward them and they fell to the floor. I saw Adam reach for their collars and smack their heads together. They were out cold.

Adam took their guns and put out his hand to help me as I jumped out of the space shuttle. "Why are you here and not homeward bound?" Adam snapped, looking left and right.

"It's been a nightmare since we left the island. Buzz collapsed and the military rushed us here to get medical help. In the confusion I lost track of my backpack with the canister and left it on the helicopter."

The news was alarming to Adam. He put his hands on top of his head and moaned, "You lost the canister I gave you!"

"But I was able to get some vials back! I went snooping around and found out where they stored the moon water."

I produced from my pocket the one vial that I still had.

"What happened next?" Adam said warily.

"While snooping around I also discovered the commander you told us about, and he wants to get rid of me and Buzz because we know all about the moon water."

Adam shook his head, not liking the news. "Is your brother still sick?"

"Not now. I gave him some moon water. I knew it would save him."

"You let your brother drink the moon water?" Adam protested.

"I had to. I didn't want him to die. It cured him like it cured you," I said, defending myself.

"Where is he?" Adam demanded.

"I don't know. I thought he was in here. Somehow we got separated. We've got to find him and get out of here."

"Let's go," Adam declared.

We took off like a search and rescue team. As precious time elapsed, I became more terrified.

Exhausted from all the mental and emotional stress, I leaned up against a wall and wiped the sweat from my forehead. A shot of adrenaline ripped through me when I heard a strange rattling noise and the wall moved behind me. I snapped around. Gazing up, my mouth fell open.

"Commando . . ." I gasped, gazing as the six-foot-tall robot rotated its hips around. The robot was shaped like a real person, with arms, legs, and a head; it instantly reminded me of my burnt up robot in the garage. But this robot was holding Buzz tight with its mechanical arms.

Adam almost toppled over me as he came to a screeching halt. Buzz was three feet off the ground and kicking his feet. One arm gripped him across his mouth and the other arm was wrapped around his waist. I pushed Adam aside, went behind the robot, opened the body, and played with different wires, buttons, and switches. Within seconds, the robot's mechanical hands had dropped Buzz to the floor.

"Stupid pile of tin!" Buzz moaned, as he punched it in the chest.

Adam was scratching his head. "I'll bet this robot plays a key role when they're in pre-launch operations," he said, rubbing his chin. "I think they program robots and put them on the launch platform to perform various technical duties. If anything dangerous goes wrong at the last minute, it's better to lose a bucket of bolts than a human life."

Cool stuff, I thought. I nodded, agreeing with Adam's deduction. I circled the robot.

"Hmmmmm, I think we might be able to use this to our advantage," I said, softly. My ingenuity was starting to kick in. "Guys, it's quite possible that we have a window of opportunity here. Buzz, I have a better idea of how to get free and this robot is perfect for my plan. It's dangerous, but it just might work!"

The Plan

"Dangerous!" Buzz exclaimed.

"It's a risky move, a shot worth taking," I insisted. "While Buzz was sick, I overheard the commander say the Secret Service will be arriving at four o'clock because the President and Vice President are going to see the next launch firsthand."

"That's great news!" Adam declared. "All we have to do is get to the Secret Service and we're home free."

"The problem is we have to stall until they get here, and the guards are fast on our tails. We need a safe place to hide."

"Any ideas?" Adam asked.

"We need a diversion, something to steer their attention away from us so we can get onto the floating launch pad. Then we can hide in the cockpit of the space shuttle until the Secret Service arrives. That's a safe place—no one would think to find us there. That's our ticket to getting saved," I said.

"Hold on, genius," Buzz protested. "How are we going to get to the launch pad?"

"The ship has lifeboats," I countered. "We get into one, lower it into the water, and paddle like there's no tomorrow."

"That launch pad must be ten stories high, Eric. How are we going to get up to the platform?" Buzz objected.

"I'm confident marine engineers built a way to get from ocean level to the platform—we won't know until we get there."

"It's an adventurous idea, but I'm a risk taker. Let's do it, kid," Adam said enthusiastically.

"Do you guarantee this plan will work?" Buzz asked, obviously not convinced.

"It's got potential," I shot back.

"Potentially dumb," Buzz grumbled, shaking his head.

"How many times have my ideas failed me, Buzz?"

"Tons," Buzz quickly answered.

Buzz was right, sometimes my ideas had failed me, but I ignored his negativity.

"Here," I said, giving Adam the map. "Search for lifeboats that we can get to."

I then focused my attention on the robot. *Just pretend that I'm back home in the garage fixing Commando. I know exactly what I'm doing,* I confidently told myself.

I opened up the back panel to examine inside. I found the function panel and the computer brain located where the heart would be in a human. There were movement power pads, energy modulation circuits, and a control box that was the microprocessor—a kind of miniaturized electronic computer for the brain. Being a whiz with connections, I rewired the movement power pads around the primary power cells. It had all sorts of red, black, and blue wires and cables, and buttons going everywhere.

"Hey, metal head, what's your name?" Buzz joked.

"Can it," I said.

"My-name-is-Titan," the robot responded in an electronic voice that came from a speaker in its mouth. Caught off guard, we all had surprised grins.

"Very, very cool!" Buzz exclaimed.

"A voice activated robot. Nice technology," I fired back.

Tinkering further with the brain, I rewired knobs and other switches, and verbally commanded Titan to move its head and arms. It performed a full range of human movements and actions.

On Titan's right mechanical arm, at the wrist, was a silver watch. The face was a compact computer screen. I took the watch off and we all looked into it. From Titan's eyes, we could see across the room— every detail was focused and in color.

"Awesome!" Buzz cheered.

"I get it," Adam said. "With this watch, engineers can see what Titan's eyes are looking at. Very impressive technology."

I strapped the cool watch to my right wrist in order

to see where Titan went and what it did. I then took the ship map back from Adam and found the fuel room where I wanted to go. With some last minute tinkering, I programmed Titan to go two hundred feet to that room.

I closed up Titan's back panel. Its eyes kept flashing red. *I'm pretty good,* I thought.

Buzz hit me in the side. "Hey, Titan, do the boogie-woogie."

"Stop goofing around, Buzz," I said, while Titan swiveled its hips around and around. Buzz grinned and gave me a thumbs-up.

"Very funny," I muttered. "We don't have time to waste dancing with a robot."

Under normal circumstances I would have enjoyed a lighthearted moment, but with our lives on the line I was shaking in my sneakers. I took the guns Adam had confiscated from the guards and placed them in the robot's mechanical hands.

"Kid, what are you doing?" Adam asked, his voice rising slightly.

"Like I said, the plan is dangerous. Now listen up, guys, there's no margin for error from here on out. I've just programmed three movements. First, Titan will head east down the corridor about one hundred steps, up the stairwell, and arrive at the rocket fuel room," I said, pointing at the map. "Step two: With its powerful machine legs, Titan will bust down the door—and then it will execute step three."

Buzz and Adam listened intently, not moving a muscle.

"This is where all the danger begins. Rocket fuel and bullets don't mix. I programmed Titan to squeeze the triggers and open fire on the tanks. If things go as planned, the bullets will cause a huge fire in the fuel room and then KABOOOM! A powerful, blazing blast will rock this ship. That's why every second is crucial. We have twelve minutes to get on that lifeboat and escape to the floating launch pad. It's a good plan because there will be total mass confusion."

"Kid, you've got a stuntman's attitude. No fear— I like it," Adam said.

"Well, I don't have a stuntman's attitude. Isn't there another plan we can go with?" Buzz moaned through chattering teeth. "Something not as life threatening . . . like finding a phone to call home?"

I shook my head. If it appeared that I had nerves of steel like Superman I was an impressive actor and deserved an Academy Award. I was just as scared as Buzz, knowing he was right, sometimes my ideas go wrong—like Commando one minute mowing the lawn, the next destroying everything in my neighborhood—and in the end I'm the big loser. My mouth was dry and my gut was spinning like I was on an out-of-control roller coaster. My knees were also shaking like an engine with leaky valves and shaky old pistons. I cleared my throat and commanded Titan to walk out the door.

"I like the plan, kid," Adam countered. "The Secret Service won't put the President in danger. With this explosion it will stir an immediate investigation."

"Yeah, but will the Secret Service show up?" Buzz asked.

Adam jumped in with his opinion. "Somebody has to investigate this explosion. It definitely is a strong plan."

I nodded, agreeing with Adam. We all watched Titan move with quick, powerful, steady steps, each stride four feet long. "Go get 'em, Robocop!" Buzz called out. What an astonishing sight Titan was with its buff chest, wide shoulders, red eyes, shiny silver body, and guns gripped in its mechanical hands.

"From here on out it's all about timing," I said.

"Just like in the movies doing stunts," Adam added enthusiastically. "This kind of action gets my adrenaline pumping."

As we watched Titan head right, we darted left scampering down the long deck. Checking around a corner, we spotted guards posted at the end of the hall. Changing directions, we made our way down the deck and found the engine room to regroup. I looked at the watch on my wrist and on the color screen I could see that Titan was moving with power and speed down the hall. So far, so good.

Just as we charged past the boilers, generators, and other machinery a deep voice shouted, "FREEZE!"

We jerked around. It was the guard Adam had

knocked out earlier. He was pointing a gun at us—we all raised our hands high. He snapped up his radio and announced with pride, "My hunch was right, I knew you'd show up sooner or later down here." Into the radio he said, "I've got them . . . all of them. We are in the engine room. Over."

"Excellent work. Stand by. Over," a gruff voice barked over the radio.

"You got away from me once, it won't happen again," the guard said, staring at Adam. "Nothing is going to save you this time."

"Stay calm, boys," Adam said with an even voice. His eyes were focused on the gun. I glanced at Buzz and his face was without expression, without emotion. He looked extremely tired, his body and emotions worn down. It was as if he had given up. Not me—I was determined to get away. My eyes shifted left and right, scanning my immediate surroundings, looking for anything I could use to my advantage. There was nothing but engine machinery. I noticed steam periodically rolling out of a pipe.

I looked up at Adam. He winked. He had a plan and I could tell that it was forceful by the fists he made. He was determined to escape and was getting ready to make his move and strike.

The guard held the gun, but the look in his eyes revealed that he was scared, uncertain of himself and wary of Adam. He did not seem like he had the guts to pull the trigger. His hand shook as he tried to keep the gun on us and he maintained a safe distance. Adam stared at the guard taking one more step. "Give me that thing before you hurt somebody."

"W-watch i-it . . ." the guard stuttered, shuffling his feet and backing up.

The guard was moving right into the pipe with the rolling steam. Adam took a small, but forceful step forward.

"Pal, don't mess with me," the guard squeaked, shaking the gun. "Or I'll . . .

I'll . . ." The guard took one more step back where a rush of white steam hit his neck.

"AAAAAAAAAAAAH!" he screamed, dropping the gun as Adam lunged and tackled the guard. They both fell backwards. The guard's head hit the boiler, knocking him out.

"That's our lucky break!" Adam exclaimed, jumping up. "Come on—guards will be here any second now because of his radio call. Let's go!"

We fled out of the engine room, toward the closest lifeboat that I found on the map. The only thing that mattered now—escape. We ran against a ticking clock, every second counting. The watch showed Titan was moving steady down the deck, but I knew my plan would fail if we didn't get to a lifeboat and get off this ship. The explosion would be as powerful as if a bomb exploded. The ship would sink fast like the Titanic. Danger, risk, high stakes—you name it; I was living life on the edge. Doom was turning out to be my middle name. As we ran the only thought that raced through me was: *Will my plan work? It's either victory or defeat . . . what is going to happen?*

CHAPTER SEVENTEEN

Crisis Situation

Running for our lives, we hustled down halls, corridors, and decks. Cautiously, we eased around a corner, and my heart dropped when I saw a pair of guards running down the hall with German shepherds.

Yikes! I was scared looking at those dogs as they barked violently.

"There they are—get 'em!" one guard shouted.

Adam grabbed us and we took off running in the opposite direction. As we zipped around the first corner, tears formed in my eyes. I knew that time was running out, that Titan was going to create a massive explosion, and the possibility of us being caught on the ship was almost bound to happen.

"New plan!" Adam hissed as he unexpectedly put on the brakes around the next corner. We were in front of a steel door. He tried the handle—it was locked.

"Need to reorganize, guys," Adam groaned. "Stay calm, kids, I work well under extreme pressure."

I could hear guards running, their pounding foot-steps getting closer. Adam gripped the handle, pressed his lips together, twisted the knob and his right arm bulged with huge muscles. The lock broke and we made it inside the room.

"Impressive brute strength you've got there, mis-ter!" Buzz proclaimed in a whisper. I remembered that it was the moon water that gave Adam his Superman strength. We stood silent, waiting, listen-ing, as the rumble of the guards went down the hall.

"That was close," Buzz rasped.

I looked at my wrist. Titan was still moving steadily up the stairs.

"Four minutes left!" Adam said, looking down at his watch. "There's no time to get onto a lifeboat and make it to the launch pad."

"Great plan, genius," Buzz snapped, pushing me in the chest. "Sure has turned out to be a real winner!"

"Cool it, kid!" Adam fired back. "I'm taking over and calling the shots from here on out! There's a way to escape before Titan fires a round of bullets."

I rubbed my aching throat. I had tears in my eyes knowing the fuel room was minutes away from blow-ing up and that there was no chance of a last-ditch effort to escape like they did in the movies.

Wiping my eyes, I caught a whiff of a strange and horrible odor coming from a wooden crate Adam was opening. Buzz smelled it too.

"What is that awful smell?" Buzz moaned.

We stepped toward two wooden crates that resembled coffins. Adam had completely opened one of the crates. We gazed down and saw a black body bag inside.

It obviously contained a corpse.

"YUCK!" exclaimed Buzz.

"Phew!" I said, holding my nose.

"Take it easy, guys. These are the others they experimented on who didn't live," Adam said, his voice trailing off. Then, with a sudden triumphant grin, Adam snapped his fingers and announced, "They're transporting them someplace. And this is how we can escape!"

"How?" Buzz and I asked together, confused.

"Hiding inside the crates!"

"WITH THE DEAD BODIES! NO WAY!" Buzz shouted.

"That's the new plan," Adam said firmly. "Now help me get these bodies out of these crates and into one of those freezers over there. I am an expert at flying choppers, and once we're in the air, I'll bust out of my crate, take out the pilot with one of my famous knockout punches, and we'll be home free. I escaped once in a helicopter; it will work again, and this time no wild storm will take us down."

"Geez," Buzz murmured, closing his eyes. He had *puke* written all over his face. "I don't like the action man's idea. Things are getting worse," he groaned, disgusted. "This is sooooo eerie, sooooo gross."

"We're running out of time and this is what we're going with," Adam said through gritted teeth. "You two move this body into the freezer." He was already working on the second crate to open it. Buzz and I looked down at the body bag and swallowed hard. I was so deep in concentration that I didn't even hear Adam until he shouted.

"NOW!" Adam barked.

Buzz and I grabbed hold of the bag and heaved the corpse into the freezer. "This is remarkable," Buzz gulped. "Remarkable."

"Remember these two code words, kids. *Superman clear*. When you hear them, you'll know I've got control of the chopper and it's safe to come out. Got it?" Adam hurriedly said.

We nodded. We continued to work together and got the other body out of the crate. As Buzz and I then moved to the empty crate, I noticed Buzz's legs were shaking.

"Do I really have to climb in?" Buzz moaned, his jaw quivering. "I feel like Dracula on Halloween. I vant your neck."

"Very funny; hop in," I muttered, pushing Buzz.

"If I live through this I'm going to have nightmares for the rest of my life, thanks to you, Eric," Buzz hissed.

He plugged his nose, and we both laid down. Adam tossed me two thumbs-up as he climbed into the other wooden crate. Before closing the lids, our eyes

met, and he said, "Hey, kid, still got the moon water?"
I nodded.

"Good, you're off the hook. Toss it to me and I'll save my friend once we get free."

With some slight hope we could survive, I froze for a second as I thought about all the money we could have that would make us rich beyond belief, all the money needed to save our Christmas tree farm. At that moment, I was confronted with the toughest decision of my life. Half of me wanted Adam to save his dying friend, but the other half wanted to keep the moon water so I could sell it and make a bunch of money and save our family business.

I struggled with my decision. I reached into my pocket and pulled out the vial. It probably weighed less than three ounces, but it felt like a couple of hefty sandbags. I imagined national headlines from newspapers all over the country: *Moon Medicine—Boy Gets Rich Finding Cure for Cancer!*

I sighed, closed my eyes, and put my hand in my pocket and felt the coin. I remembered my wish: I really wanted a million dollars. This was my big chance to get it . . . but what was the correct choice to make? With all the inner strength I could muster, I fought off the temptation to keep the moon water and told myself I was going to do the right thing: The vial could give someone a second chance at life.

"Hey, kid, snap out of it!" Adam ordered, holding out his hand. "Hurry!"

I popped open my eyes, ready to toss the vial over to Adam whose arm stretched out like he was trying to catch a ball at a baseball game. Voices were at the door, and we both dropped down into the crates, closing the lids. Buzz and I froze like corpses when we heard the guards talking.

"We're in a crisis situation!" one voice exclaimed. "The Secret Service is here. Commander Evans wants these bodies off this ship, now!"

"What's the plan, sir?"

"A pilot from Headquarters has orders to take all the crates of moon water and the bodies back to the mainland. The only setback is that pilot flew in a smaller helicopter, now there's not enough room for both bodies and the ten crates of moon water. One body will go in the chopper; the other one, that's a different story."

"What are we going to do?" the other voice asked.

"Get rid of it—take it to the launch pad and drop it. The Secret Service will never find it there. Let's move!"

Buzz and I were alarmed. *Get rid of it . . . the launch pad . . .* I said to myself. *Oh no, we are getting separated from Adam! Which crate is going where? What do we do now?*

I wanted to scream, but I didn't dare. Instead, I just wanted to cry, let out all the tension and fear that had built up inside. Every move we made seemed to become a worse nightmare. Panic gripped me by the throat and it was taking me down into the depths of the sea with no hope I would survive. *How in the world are we going to get out of this pickle?*

CHAPTER EIGHTEEN

Stress to the Max

As we were whisked down the hall, I was frightened. I racked my brain for a way to get out of the predicament. I swallowed hard, knowing the possibility of getting free was hopelessly bleak.

I knew when we hit the top deck of the ship because I heard the thundering noise of the helicopter blades spinning. A big jolt told me we'd been tossed inside the chopper.

"GO!" someone barked just as a door slammed shut. In seconds we were off and I didn't know in which direction we were heading, to the floating launch pad or back to headquarters.

Up and away, the helicopter tilted at a forty-five degree angle and departed from the ship. My heart beat like a drum. I glanced down at the watch on my wrist and saw that Titan had arrived at the stairwell leading to the fuel room. It stopped and I saw white smoke that appeared to be rising up from its metal body. Having performed numerous repairs on my own robot, I had a gut feeling one of the main fuses inside its wiring system had blown, creating a malfunction. Translation: Fire!

Titan moved upward and began to climb the stairs as more smoke rose from its body. The smoke was getting thicker by the moment and I knew all too well it had a serious electrical problem, and the worst part of it was there was nothing I could do but watch. Its movements were jerky, but Titan successfully reached the top of the stairwell. With my eyes locked on the robot, the transmission went blank.

"Oh, no," I moaned, hitting the watch.

The watch flickered, and instead of color images appearing on the watch, they were black-and-white. Somehow, I was able to follow Titan's movements as the screen faded in and out. With its powerful metal legs it crushed down the door and took two steps in as more smoke billowed out from its body. Titan's head started to spin around and around, and spun so fast it popped off and dropped to the floor.

"Oh, no," I moaned again.

Things were really going haywire. The black-and-white pictures faded and color images again appeared. The color wasn't sharp, but somewhat fuzzy; I don't know how, but I was able to make out what was going on.

Titan's head stopped spinning on the floor and its eyes were pointed upward. I saw red, white, and blue sparks flying from its decapitated chest like a fireworks show on the Fourth of July. Then, from the waist up, its metal frame exploded in a wild blaze of fire and sizzling sparks shot high into the air from its neck. With one last surge of power, Titan's body took one final step forward to stand up against a silver fuel tank. Its whole body, from shoulders to feet, was engulfed in flames.

I watched, stunned, knowing that Titan was on the verge of exploding. I felt the helicopter dip; it felt like we were descending. The crate shifted and we slid a few feet. Frozen, listening, waiting to see what would happen next, Buzz said in a harsh whisper, "This stinks!"

"Got that right," I agreed.

"How are we going to get out of this one?" Buzz said desperately.

I had no idea and didn't know what to say. All I wanted to do was cry an ocean of tears then crawl into a cave.

Just then I felt another jolt, and the trip came to an end. No longer were we blazing through the sky. We had touched down and I knew where we were because of the short trip—on the floating launch pad. I heard the helicopter door snap open and a gruff voice shout again, "GO!"

The crate was lifted up and I heard another voice ask frantically, "Where do you want this thing dumped?"

"Here!" a voice cried out.

We dropped with a thud and my heart sank. My

shirt was soaked with sweat. The helicopter raced its engines, accelerated its blades, and then took off. With our hands shaking, Buzz and I cracked the lid and stood up. Stunned, we saw the towering space shuttle, with white steam shooting out from its engines, a short distance away. We both gulped.

"Uh oh!" Buzz exclaimed.

I gazed upward in awe at the two huge rocket boosters and gigantic orange fuel tank connected to the space shuttle. Even under the dreadful and stressful circumstances, it was still an awesome sight to behold so close up.

"Bro . . . what are the odds of this thing being launched?" Buzz asked faintly.

"Uh . . . pretty doggoned good," I declared with fear.

We both leaped out of the crate and I couldn't believe I was actually standing on top of the floating launch platform. Waves rolled in the sea and I was amazed at how motionless the platform was. I looked over at Buzz—his eyes were huge and terror was written all over his face.

"ERIC! WE'VE GOT TO GET OFF THIS THING OR WE'RE GOING TO DIE WHEN THE SHUTTLE BLASTS OFF!"

He was right. The launch pad was at least forty yards wide and perhaps ten stories high. The only way I saw to save our lives was to jump off. Just as I was ready to tell Buzz that, a sudden thought struck me: Sharks!

Buzz hit me in the shoulder and pointed—overhead we saw a helicopter flying away. My mouth went dry. My heart sank to the bottom of my gut when I realized that inside that helicopter Adam was minutes away from being safe and free. He would successfully escape without us.

I looked at Buzz and, without him saying a word, I knew his feelings. It was in his face, the fear in his eyes. This was the end.

I glanced down at the watch and I saw that Titan was still engulfed in a yellow ball of fire. Buzz leaned forward and together it was an astonishing site watching Titan spew fire from its metal frame. Any second it was going to. . . .

KABOOOMMMMMMMM!

Buzz and I fell backwards a few feet. The ship, a hundred yards away, jolted upward and sprayed chunks of steel out into the ocean—it was as if a giant bomb had just gone off. A twenty-five-foot hole appeared in the hull of the ship and it began to sink fast. Crew members scrambled on the top deck.

"EVERYONE FOR LIFEBOATS!" a panicked voice shouted over the ship's speakers. Alarms were blaring, black smoke was rising, and flames were shooting from the hole.

A horn in the shuttle blew so loud that I thought it had snapped my eardrums. Plugging our ears, Buzz and I turned and gazed up at the shuttle. A door flew open and two astronauts leaped out, descended ten stories down, and landed on a rubber raft that launched into the air—all those days of training for an emergency had paid off. That special rubber jet boat instantly shot them fifty feet out into the ocean. As soon as they hit the water, it was pedal to the metal. Talk about an awesome getaway. I felt like I was standing in the middle of a stunt show at Universal Studios!

GET OFF OF THIS LAUNCH PAD OR YOU'LL BE BLOWN AWAY! THE SHUTTLE'S GOING TO LAUNCH! I warned myself.

I grabbed Buzz by the arm and jerked him. As we turned to run, shadowy figures moved out from a crane. Two robots were coming toward us with out-stretched mechanical arms.

Buzz and I scrambled away from the pair of moving metal beings and darted into the open elevator where I frantically started pushing buttons. Just as the robots were close enough to grab us with their mechanical hands, the door closed, sending the elevator climbing higher, higher, and higher.

Seconds later it came to a halt, and we jumped out to find ourselves inside the cockpit of the space shuttle. The elevator door shut. There must have been hundreds of buttons and switches all over the place. I felt like I was in the cockpit of an airliner.

"BUZZ—LOOK!" I yelled, pointing to a computer screen right in front of us. It had numbers counting down: 60 . . . 59 . . . 58. . . .

My eyes and jaw flew open at the same time. Buzz and I stared at each other and he screamed, "WE'RE GOING TO BLAST OFF!"

"Stay calm, Buzz. Panic makes the situation worse, not better," I warned.

My eyes moved lightning fast, scanning the instrument panel. I looked at the countdown clock, seeing the numbers flash: 48 . . . 47 . . . 46. . . .

"We've got to escape like those astronauts!" Buzz yelped.

He moved to the shuttle door and jerked the handle, but it would not open. He jerked it again and again.

"ERIC, WE'RE STUCK. THE DOOR—IT WON'T OPEN!"

A digital voice sounded over a loudspeaker: "Thirty seconds and counting. Onboard computers are go for launch."

Out of the corner of my eye I saw a red button. Under it were the words: **MAIN ENGINES CUT-OFF SYSTEM.** I hit the button. I gazed down at the countdown clock: 29 . . . 28 . . . 27. . . .

"Something's wrong with the computer—it won't shut down! Everything's frozen!" I cried out, my voice shaking.

"What in the world!" Buzz groaned, looking out a window.

I looked out the shuttle windshield and I couldn't believe what I was seeing! "BUBBLES?" I exclaimed, stunned by the sight of millions of tiny white bubbles. They were floating up in the air. I felt my legs buckle and I fell backward into an astronaut seat.

"ERIC, YOU SCREWED UP THE ENGINES WHEN YOU PUT DETERGENT IN THE FUEL! YOU DID THIS! NOW WE'RE DEAD MEAT! NICE MESS YOU GOT US INTO!" Buzz shouted, glaring at me.

I looked at the instrument panel and saw an eight-inch color screen in front of us displaying the space shuttle's boosters. My mouth hung wide open as I watched endless bubbles shoot out of the burning boosters. *What an epic disaster!* I grumbled to myself. *What have I done?*

I looked down at the countdown clock and saw that the numbers were continuing to count down: 10 . . . 9 . . . 8. . . .

We looked at each other. Terror leaped from our eyes. One blink later, speechless, we both looked away thinking the same thought, and we quickly strapped on the seat belts as the digital voice came over the loudspeaker again: "Main boosters are igniting. We are go for launch in five . . . four. . . ."

Buzz put his hands over his eyes as the digital voice delivered the final countdown.

"Three . . . two . . . one."

KABOOOOOOOOOM!

The space shuttle shook so hard, I thought my teeth would fly out.

"AHHHHHHHHHHHHH!" Buzz and I screamed together, grasping hands.

Millions of pounds of rocket fuel ignited in the engines. I watched the computer screen, and the bubbles burst, soaking everyone in the lifeboats with soapy water as we roared away. Suds swirled in the crashing waves created by the liftoff, making the ocean look like one big bubble bath party.

My bones shook as we traveled at 3,000 miles per hour in a tower of metal racing toward space. The high speed peeled the skin back on our faces.

I glanced down at the panel, which was covered with instruments and complex computers. They were spitting out numbers so rapidly that I couldn't even see what they were. All I knew was we were hauling super-duper fast. Scared to the max, I had one thought that kept racing over and over in my mind: *Is this the end?*

CHAPTER NINETEEN

Guts

BOOOOOOM!

The bang was so loud that it made my heart drop a thousand feet and I thought that a fire was about to start from the engines. I gripped my shaking seat as it vibrated from the powerful force of the thundering engines. My body was shaking so hard I thought my bones were going to snap.

Shaking, waiting, listening, I felt the space shuttle stop its sharp climb toward outer space and begin to level out. Buzz and I gazed out the windshield and saw that we were streaking across the sky like a blazing comet. Still puzzled about what had just happened, I saw something blinking on one of the control panel's monitors. I realized that it was a status message—the main boosters had separated from the shuttle.

To my left was a small window. I saw nothing but the deep blue ocean below, along with some brown specks of islands that we zinged past. I turned to Buzz and he grunted, "What are we going to do?"

Silence.

Staring at the space shuttle instruments I sighed. *I'm pretty good with computers and electronics, but this stuff . . . it's out of my league,* I thought, searching hard for something that I might recognize.

"Got any good news?" Buzz asked in a faint voice.

I paused, "Well, we've got enough fuel to go around the world ten times!"

Buzz smirked, then leaned his head back against the leather seat. I sat there studying the instruments. A computer screen flashed the words: **Alert. Engine failure. Shuttle re-routing to Area-1 for emergency landing.**

"What is going on, Eric?" Buzz said, pointing to the computer screen. "What does that mean?"

Pausing, thinking before I answered, it occurred to me that NASA engineers had pre-programmed the space shuttle to land in a designated area if the engine had a malfunction.

Just as I was getting ready to answer Buzz with my observation, smoke shot out of the nose of the shuttle. *Yikes! Smoke means fire!*

"Buzz, we've got a huge problem!" I yelled.

"The shuttle, it's on fire! Do something!" Buzz lashed out.

"Oh, boy," I muttered, wiping beads of sweat from my forehead. *What can I do?*

I noticed a small compartment. Opening it, I found a bunch of charts with all sorts of numbers and graphics. I pulled them out, seeing what looked like high-tech space geometry or something. *Way too advanced for me.* Those charts were over my head and too confusing for my brain.

Discouraged, I tossed the charts down. Buzz looked at me and cried with despair, "We're going to crash and die; it's just a matter of time!"

I covered my eyes not wanting Buzz to be right. When I looked again, more smoke was coming from the nose of the space shuttle. With all the emotional strength I had left, I fought off the sinking thoughts of defeat.

Over and over I kept telling myself, *Don't give up or give in, Eric. Determination is the key to victory.* With good old-fashioned grit, I adjusted the seat belt and focused on the task at hand: Getting us out of our pitiful dilemma.

The most important thing was to relax, so I closed my eyes again. I could feel my jaw tightening up from all the stress that was building from within. Loosening it, I visualized the schoolbooks that I had brought home from the library and remembered building my mini space shuttle in the garage. I remembered studying how the big boys at NASA made their rockets, and how I had successfully made my space shuttle and launched it from my launch pad floating in the school pool. I could see the chapters right before my eyes—everything from launch and flight operations to engine thrust control. I wanted to kick myself for not reading the chapter on the emergency crew escape system, but never in my wildest dreams could I have thought at the time that I would one day travel in a real space shuttle with death knocking at my door.

Seconds ticked by, and I remembered the chapter on the main landing gears. Because I was creative and had wanted to earn points from my peers for style, I had ditched the idea of landing my space shuttle like an airplane, like shuttles do when they leave orbit and re-enter the atmosphere from missions. Rather, I had gone with a more creative approach: I had designed my space shuttle so that it could land in the water. Even there in the cockpit I could still hear the cheers all my friends gave me when I triumphantly brought my own shuttle in for a memorable splashdown.

Just then, I felt goose bumps prickle on my arms. A brilliant thought struck my brain. I was onto something huge. I had a strong hunch that NASA engineers were capable of landing space shuttles in the water just like I had done with mine. *Wow,* I thought gulping hard. *I'm really, really onto something. If they launch space shuttles from the ocean, they must bring them back down into the water!* I had come up with something that actually could be used in real life!

Up against the crisis of my life, I felt sweat roll down my armpits. I focused on getting the space shuttle into a nosedive position and somehow getting the parachutes to release so that we could crash into the sea without demolishing the shuttle—or even worse, killing us.

"Buzz," I called, "I think I'm onto something!"

Reading his body language, I saw the weight of the world lift itself from his shoulders and a ray of hope that we could survive dimly glow from his weary eyes.

"You've always had the knack for clutch plays, and if anyone can save us, you can, bro," he confidently told me.

My eyes focused on the computer console. It was jam-packed with buttons, switches, and computers. Completely overwhelmed, I sat gazing at the console.

"Eric, the plan . . ." Buzz rattled.

"Cut the engines so the shuttle goes into a nose-dive position."

"Nosedive position!"

"Buzz, if I can rig my space shuttle to land in the water so that it doesn't shatter, so can the military. Trust me, Buzz, this plan's a winner."

"But yours was a homemade mini model toy!"

"That's where experiments start!"

Buzz sputtered nervously. "Y-you're serious . . . y-you're going to attempt to land this thing in the ocean?"

"If I can do it, so can hot-shot NASA engineers!" I proclaimed with confidence.

"You've got big guts," Buzz muttered, covering his face with his hands.

I gazed around the console, concentrating, again looking at the mechanisms. A screen flashed red, green, and then yellow. I had no idea what that meant, but it was cool. I felt like I was an astronaut, and this was my space shuttle, and a successful splashdown was my mission and challenge. I looked around the cockpit and got comfortable in the leather seat.

"Time to get to work," I said with nerves of steel. "Now, how do astronauts cut the engines?"

"Beats me, I'm useless with technology," Buzz groaned. "That's your department."

Staring at a cluster of buttons and switches, I recalled the chapter in my schoolbook about the onboard computer system and how it functioned. Whether in a car, a boat, a plane, or a rocket, the key to all engines was electricity. I looked for something of that sort and saw a series of black switches that read: ELECTRICAL POWER SUPPLY, MAIN IGNITION UNIT, and MASTER PROPULSION SYSTEM. A lump the size of an orange was lodged in my throat and I had to swallow twice to get it down. With all the guts I possessed, I leaned forward, hand shaking, and flipped all the switches. Crossing my fingers, hoping I did the right thing, I saw numbers on a computer screen racing backward. Two blinks later, the space shuttle engines sputtered and then popped. I looked at the altitude vertical director—we had begun to drop.

Buzz's eyes grew large as the front of the shuttle tilted downward and we started to descend. We both looked out the windshield and saw land—a vast amount of it.

"Oh no, you stupid dope!" Buzz screamed. "You blew it . . . you cut power while we're over land!"

Sweat pouring down my forehead, I felt myself choking under the extreme pressure. My brain was doing loop-the-loops inside my head and I had to think fast to get us out of this deadly situation. The shuttle was now in the position I wanted and was charging straight down, like a pelican diving headfirst into the water for food. Except where was the water?

"DO SOMETHING, ERIC!" Buzz lashed out. "NOW!"

Think! I shouted to myself inside my head. *Think like an astronaut who's an expert at crisis situations.* Squeezing my eyes shut, I visualized myself flying my mini shuttle in the neighborhood. So many times I had lost control of it, dooming it to crash into homes or trees. Under those stressful conditions, not wanting to have to go back to the old drawing board and rebuild my shuttle, I had always attempted to safely glide it back to earth and land it on the street. It was the difficulty of doing it that had helped me come up with the idea to drop the shuttle into the school swimming pool.

My eyes instantly popped open. If I could gain control of the shuttle and get us turned around, I might be able to glide us out over the ocean and skillfully drop us into the rough ocean swells below, escaping death.

Remaining unwavering in my determination to save Buzz's life and mine, I grabbed hold of the black joystick in front of me and gripped it hard. I felt like a fighter pilot in a virtual game, watching the earth below getting closer and closer. Desperately, I pulled back the stick, and the space shuttle began to lift a few degrees.

"YESSSSSSSSS!" Buzz shouted.

Buzz put his sweaty hands on top of mine, and we pulled on the stick with a firm grip, gritting our teeth. Miraculously, the space shuttle rose from its dive and leveled out.

The shuttle seemed light in the air as we glided it in the clear blue sky. Breathing like I had just completed a marathon, I looked at Buzz. He shook his head, exhaled a huge sigh of relief, and muttered, "That's a miracle!"

He removed his hands from mine as I moved the joystick forward and backward, delicately maneuvering the flying machine. I calmed my breathing, looked out the windshield, and saw the ocean below. My next move was daring, adventurous, and perilous. With my lips pressed together, I pushed the joystick forward. Again the space shuttle tilted downward, descending in a nosedive.

"NOOOOOOOOOOOOO!" Buzz wailed, overcome with dread.

With the joystick clutched in my palm, I felt like a bomber engaged in battle and I was flying into hostile territory. Trembling, I rapidly scanned the console for the button or switch to release the main parachute. It was impossible to tell which one it was, so I hit all of them.

We were falling fast and my brain was flipping out in the perilous drop. Buzz covered his eyes with his hands, and I crossed my fingers, hoping that the parachute would open. Two heartbeats later, we felt a huge jolt. It was so powerful that it shot us forward. On the computer monitor, a large red, white, and blue parachute blossomed on the screen.

"Buzz, look!"

As stunned as I was, he gazed at the monitor.

"Yessssssssss!" I howled with a triumphant grin.

In a controlled fall, floating downward, we watched the ocean get closer—in seconds this was going to be one thrashing splashdown into the crashing waves. We clutched ourselves in our seats, bracing our bodies for the bone-crushing jolt of a lifetime!

"If this works, Eric . . . you're a genius," Buzz muttered.

"Brace for impact!"

The ocean got larger and larger by the seconds. "Oh, boy . . . Oh, boy . . ." I dug my fingernails into the leather seat.

WHAOOOOOMMMM!

Our heads whipped forward as we hit the ocean

with great force and we went down into the sea. My nails dug deeper into the seat as the shuttle spun around in circles. I was getting dizzy and my stomach was spinning out of control along with my brain. I opened one eye and looked out, all I could see were white bubbles floating upward—I was relieved to know that they didn't come from soap this time. Seconds later we stopped spinning and I blinked my eyes numerous times. Checking out our bodies, we found no broken bones. The shuttle was slowly drifting toward the surface.

"We made it! We made it! That was so awesome!" I cried out.

"Eric, you did it!" Buzz cheered, shaking me. "This was the wackiest ride of my life!"

I nodded, agreeing with Buzz. It definitely had been the most awesome ride we had ever had. Once Mom and Dad took us to Roller Coaster City theme park, and I thought they had the greatest rides in the world—no way. This one ruled!

When we got to the surface, we felt a solid bump, knowing we must have hit something. We had safely made it back on dry land and I couldn't wait to pop open the shuttle door to see where we had landed. We unfastened our seat belts, shot out of our seats, and opened the door. We hopped out and gasped at the same time. Stunned and surprised, Buzz and I looked at each other in complete disbelief. Never in a million years would anyone guess where we'd landed!

CHAPTER TWENTY

The Promise

The sun was gently lowering into the ocean and small clouds of fog were rolling in with the cool breeze. Boats were sailing around and seagulls were circling in the sky.

"H-huh?" Buzz sputtered, with his mouth hanging open.

We both blinked several times. It was such a startling discovery.

"How could this be?" I asked.

I remembered the main computer terminal in the space shuttle and the message: **alert, engine failure, shuttle re-routing to Area-1 for emergency landing.** *This is where Area-1 is located.*

We were now on the shore of a white, sandy beach with people of all ages starting to charge over. All I could hear was one big mumble as they fired out questions at me and Buzz. Admittedly, it wasn't every day they saw a space shuttle splash down in the ocean and two kids pop out. It had to be an all-time first.

Buzz and I looked around and then shot each other surprised looks. I pinched myself to make sure I wasn't dreaming, then raised my arms in triumph. Thrilled that something had finally gone right, I gazed up at the Golden Gate Bridge. My thoughts raced home to Mom, Dad, and Pugsly.

"We're in San Francisco, Eric!" Buzz roared.

"How in the world did that happen?" I gasped.

"Who cares? We're back on dry land and closer to home," Buzz declared.

I just shook my head, stunned at how the events had turned out. As I looked out, more onlookers charged over to gaze at us like we were aliens who had landed on Earth. I felt like saying, "Take me to your leader."

A little girl with a runny nose looked up at her mother and said eagerly, "Mommy, I want to ride that ride. Where's the line?"

Buzz hit me in the shoulder. "Let's get out of here before television news crews get here."

I caught Buzz's drift. Just then, a traffic cop rushed down the slope and exclaimed into a small black handheld radio, "It's two kids getting out of a space shuttle! Hey boys, come here!"

Buzz and I didn't want to answer any questions. We zipped past the cop and zigzagged our way past the crowd, making our way to one of San Francisco's busiest tourist attractions, where people from all over the world go to shop, eat, and find entertainment:

Fisherman's Wharf. Out of breath, we finally stopped running and stood next to a rail overlooking the docks.

Thrilled that we were safe, Buzz enthusiastically cheered, shaking me, "Yes! It's over!"

He was so happy, he shook his hips and did a dance like the pro football players do when they score a touchdown. I was excited, but not as zealous as Buzz. I calmly looked at my brother and said, "Sorry to bring you bad news, but there's no time for a victory dance."

Buzz's mood instantly changed. His bright smile turned to a frown and he stopped wiggling his hips. "What's that supposed to mean?"

"We have some unfinished business," I said, pulling the vial of moon water out of my pocket along with the picture of Julie Johnson. I looked around, making sure no one was listening. "Buzz, I've got to make good on the promise," I said. "I promised Adam that I would get to San Francisco to save Julie—and here I am."

A fiery glare appeared in Buzz's eyes. "Oh, give me a break. I just had a good dose of terror, along with several near-death experiences, and the last thing I need is one more brain-splitter!" Buzz snipped, poking me in the chest. "Don't tell me you're serious and want to get that moon water to her?"

I needed to think about each word before I said it. I cleared my throat and announced, "Buzz, honesty is the best policy."

Buzz was silent, but his face said it all. I could read him like a book. If this had been the beginning chapter, I'd have called it *Sour Grapes.*

"Oh, don't preach to me, you blockhead. Promises are overrated. You don't have to keep them."

"Yes you do!" I said, standing my ground. "A promise is a promise and I keep mine. Now's not the time to develop a sore attitude."

"I don't have a sore attitude."

"Oh yeah? Just acting like you don't have a sore attitude makes you guilty of having one."

"Well, I guess I've got one. What are you going to do about it?" Buzz pushed back.

At that point my brother was in a fistfight mood, and whenever that happened, I always ended up the big loser.

"You're nothing but trouble," I said, shaking the vial.

All of a sudden, Buzz's eyes lit up like fireworks. His mood shifted like the wind. "Wait a minute, let me see that vial." Buzz said, wide eyed.

I tried to speak, knowing that Buzz was up to something, but he cut me off, putting his arm across my shoulders.

"You know, that's actually great, bro—this is beautiful!" Buzz howled. He then snatched the vial from my hand and held it up like it was a trophy.

"Give it back," I snapped.

"Nope," Buzz said, pushing me away as I tried to reach up for it.

"Stop being cruel and hand it over."

"Nope."

"Buzz, you're a menace."

"I'm going to be a rich menace, too! Ever hear the expression: *I laughed all the way to the bank?*"

"Buzz, we can't sell it. That's not the right thing to do. That girl needs that stuff. It will cure her!"

"Blah, blah, blah. This stuff will make us rich!"

Wrong choice, I thought to myself as I slumped over a rail. A row of sailboats were tied up along the dock. An elderly man with white hair was snoozing while a dog and a fishing pole rested by his side. In the calm water below my image reflected off the water. I watched it, and it was as if time stood still.

I found my thoughts drifting. The peacefully snoozing man reminded me of Uncle Milo. I looked out over the ocean. Something deep in my gut made me feel certain that Uncle Milo had survived that wild storm. The sea was his life and he'd been exposed to treacherous storms before. I just didn't feel it was his time to go. But I wished I knew for sure.

Buzz leaned over the rail and spit. A giant loogie landed on the reflection of my face in the water.

"Perfect shot," Buzz chuckled.

I looked at Buzz. He was looking at the vial like it was gold in the palm of his hands.

"The way I look at it, Eric," Buzz said. "Somebody is going to fork out the big bucks for this stuff and we'll be in the money. Lots of it!"

My greedy brother raised his eye brows up and down and then dashed off, vanishing into the heart of Fisherman's Wharf. Chasing after him, I got trapped behind a slow-moving group of tourists snapping photographs.

Maneuvering past them, I stopped at a fish shop and almost puked at the smell of raw fish, shark, crab, shrimp, squid, and octopus. I had to plug my nose to block the nasty odor of their dead guts. *I sure wasn't cut out to be a fisherman*, I thought. The tour group saw me plugging my nose and pointed, giggling, and took my picture.

"Very funny," I muttered.

Ignoring them, I turned away. Still holding my nose, I hoped to spot a clue which would lead me to Buzz. My ears shot up like a dog responding to a high pitched whistle. Shop merchants shouted in different foreign languages. One man shouted at the top of his lungs in English, "POLICE! STOP THAT MAN, HE'S STEALING SQUIDS!"

Two plainclothes security guards turned to see a man sprinting away with a box under his arm and they immediately pulled radios from their jackets. To my surprise, Buzz jumped up from behind a boiler of crabs. From my angle, I could see the squid thief was running right into a trap. My eyes froze on Buzz as the two men prepared to toss a net on the thief as he charged by.

Buzz moved, putting himself in the wrong place at

the wrong time. The net landed perfectly on the man, who stumbled, lost his balance, and rammed right into Buzz. Together they fell into a large tub of live lobsters with active pincers. "AAAAAAAAAAAH!" Buzz shouted at the top of his lungs.

The security guards ran over, jerked Buzz up, and pulled two large lobsters from the seat of his pants. Pain was written all over his face. Hustling my way over to Buzz, I snapped the vial out of his hand exclaiming, "See what kind of trouble greed will get you into?"

"That's going to leave a mark," Buzz grumbled, rubbing the spot where the lobsters had been. I grabbed him and pulled him away. When I turned I saw a tourist map of San Francisco pasted on a display board. I looked at the picture that Adam gave me of Julie and turned over the photograph, which had the address on the back. I studied the map carefully, found the street I needed, and led Buzz out of Fisherman's Wharf.

"Come on, Buzz. It's time to bring this comic book adventure to a close."

Shoulders slumped, head down, Buzz groaned, "That's the all-time best thing I've heard since I've been on this trip. I'm sick of smelling fish guts. What do we do now?"

"Keep our eyes focused on the finish line. I can smell victory. We're going to be heroes!"

CHAPTER TWENTY-ONE

Mission Accomplished

My feet stumbled along as Buzz and I walked, flat-out fatigued, for blocks up the hilly street. My body was running out of steam, and on top of that I had a headache pounding my brain. I looked at the picture that Adam had given me of his dying friend and wondered if Julie was still alive as we continued up the steep streets. The odds were slim, only time would tell.

Judging from the map at Fisherman's Wharf, I guessed that the street I was aiming for was only a few blocks away. Just as I was ready to announce to Buzz that we were almost there, he grabbed me by the arm and said, "Hey, I just thought of something."

"What," I groaned, stopping at the curb.

"Remember when we were inside the crate and a guard grumbled over the size of the helicopter? He said the pilot flew in the wrong-sized chopper."

I searched my memory, recalled that moment, and nodded.

"The guards then took the crate that action man was in along with the crates of moon water."

"Yeah, what's your point?"

"My point is, action man was around those vials of moon water in the helicopter. It's quite possible that he escaped and made off with all the moon water he wanted. From there, he could work his way to San Francisco and save the girl himself. We're off the hook. We shouldn't have to do this!" Buzz said, tapping me on the chest.

Buzz had an impressive point. I looked down at the pavement and computed those facts inside my brain.

"Good deduction on my part," Buzz bragged.

"No doubt he could escape and make off with vials of moon water, but there are too many what ifs—something could go wrong. What if he got away, but by the time he finally got here, the girl's dead because he was too late to get to her? What if the helicopter had engine problems and it crashed in the ocean; who'd save the girl?"

"You watch too many movies." Buzz scowled.

"Don't get me wrong, Buzz, I want the money. But if something happened to that guy and it was all up to me, I'd say that it would then be our duty to pull through and save the girl."

"Whatever . . ." Buzz scowled again. "All I've got to say is if she's history, we're in the money. Let's go."

"That's fair," I said as we crossed the street. "We've got to at least try."

As we walked the last few blocks, my thoughts went to our family business. In the event we saved Julie, we also lost the Christmas tree farm. *Boy, that's a tough one to swallow,* I thought. I felt depressed. Just how had I managed to get myself into this position? The only thing I could think of was the coin and the wish that tossed me into this wild adventure. Not wanting to dwell on that fact, I dismissed all those thoughts. I knew that saving someone's life was the noblest thing on the planet, and that's what I was going to do.

I came to a halt. We had arrived at the street that would lead us to her. A short distance away I spotted a sign on a tall, white, Victorian home. It read: SAINT MARTIN'S REST HOME. I looked at the picture Adam gave me and checked the address. I glanced at the mailbox.

"That's it! That's the place, Buzz. See? 310 Washington Street. The address on the back of the picture confirms it."

The three-story house was sandwiched between other homes of the same type. It had zippo yard, two small potted flowers on the doorstep, and a white mailbox with a small United States of America flag next to it. We walked up to the white picket fence and found the gate open, so we strolled in and made our way to the front door. With a lump in my throat, I rang the doorbell and heard the chimes sound clearly.

The door opened and a nurse greeted us with a friendly voice. "May I help you?"

I cleared my throat and replied, "Yes, we're here to see Julie Johnson."

"I'm sorry, but visiting hours are over. Come back tomorrow," she said, closing the door.

I shot a surprised look at Buzz. "Tomorrow . . . that means she's alive."

"I heard," Buzz mumbled, snapping his fingers. "Goodbye cash-oh-la."

We walked down the path and moved onto the street. I put my hands on my hips and looked up at the home.

"Eric, you're thinking something; that's not good."

"We've got to push up the agenda. We're not coming back tomorrow. I want to go home. Come on, I see a gate leading to the back."

"What are you getting us into now?" Buzz whispered.

"Be quiet . . . I'm thinking."

The sun set and darkness started to loom. I'd never broken into a home before, but the only thing on my mind was to accomplish my mission and save the girl.

"Eric, can't we just forget it?" Buzz murmured.

"Nope."

"I don't have a good feeling about this," Buzz moaned.

"I do."

In the dark, we crept our way to the back door. Just then a beam of light from a flashlight caught Buzz and I off guard as it hit our guilty faces.

"Hey, you boys robbing us?" an old man said, shaking a fist.

"Ahhhh . . . no sir . . . we're not criminals. Honest!"
Buzz said, hitting me in the side, which translated to:
I do all the talking.

"We . . . just . . . want to leave a surprise for Julie
Johnson and make sure she gets it," Buzz said with
confidence.

"Tomorrow's her birthday. Is that what this is all
about?" the man said.

"U-uh, y-yeah, that's it. One big s-surprise!"
I sputtered while nodding.

"Okay, make it snappy. Them nurses catch you and
you'll be spending the night behind bars."

I was eager to know who this old man was.
I decided to take the conversation further before we
all tiptoed in and he separated from us.

"Do you live here?" I asked.

"Unfortunately, I'm a patient. But at night I like to
have a little fun, and I got a system so I can sneak out
for a quick milk run. You know, treats and sweets," he
said with a wink, showing us a bag of peanut M&Ms.
"Them mean nurses won't let anyone eat after dinner."

"Cool system. I dig it." Buzz grinned.

"Okay, boys. Get inside and make it snappy," the
old man ordered.

We all shuffled in not making a peep. Not one
creak in the wooden floor as we tip-toed along like cat
burglars.

"Go up the stairs and down the hall. She's in Room
212. Good luck, boys," the old man whispered.

"I feel like a thief," Buzz whispered.

"Sssshh!"

"This is nuts, Eric."

"Sssshh!"

As we tip-toed down the hall, the only sounds were loud TVs in closed rooms. My eyes were on high alert as I studied each door.

"Yes! 212," I whispered, pointing to a door slightly open.

We could hear teeth being brushed in a bathroom from another door slightly open as I peered in. From behind us we heard footsteps walking up the stairs. *Someone's coming!* Buzz and I dashed in and darted to the closet to hide. What a lucky break. Julie never heard us.

"I can't believe we're doing this—it's crazy," Buzz whispered.

Ignoring him, I cracked the closet door and peeped out. On Julie's bed stand I saw a white candle burning; next to it there was a picture of Adam. She walked in wearing a red robe. She was petite with auburn hair, gentle blue eyes, and she looked thin and weary. There were lines under her eyes. Maybe from stress or the cancer. Maybe both.

I pulled the door, leaving just a thin crack to peep out of. *How can I do this? I can't just pop out and deliver the goods. She'll scream her head off and Buzz and I will end up in jail. Think, Eric . . . what can you do?*

I noticed that she had a glass of water on the night-stand. She got up from the bed and went back to the bathroom. That was my big break. I shot out of the closet to the nightstand. I opened the vial and, with my hand trembling, poured the moon water into the glass. I then rushed back to the closet.

"Mission accomplished," I muttered to Buzz.

"You've got guts, bro. Mighty big guts."

When Julie came back, she sat on the edge of the bed, looked into the candle flame, and sighed, turning her attention to the picture of Adam. Holding it, her lips trembled slightly, and a tear rolled down her cheek.

This must be a nightly thing, I said to myself.

She then put the picture down and picked up the glass of water.

"This is it," Buzz muttered, hitting me in the ribs.

She raised the glass to her lips. My heart was pounding like a drum at a rock concert.

"Come on...come on..." I urged in a faint whisper.

She swallowed a few sips, and Buzz and I each took a deep breath . . . and held it, knowing what would happen next. Her nose started to turn beet red like Rudolph the Red-Nosed Reindeer. Noticing her glowing nose in a mirror on the wall, she shot up, and with great shock she watched her eyes glow orange, green, then blue.

"Oh-my-gosh! It's happening!" Buzz cried out in a sharp whisper.

She coughed and her fingers flashed hot pink. Her arms turned bright yellow, then black, then yellow again, with purple stripes streaking down her right arm, stopping at the wrist. In response to the bizarre happenings, she got ready to do what I would have done—scream. But she couldn't—she'd lost her breath. Falling to the bed, she began to choke, kick her legs, and toss her head back and forth.

"Oh no . . . something's wrong!" I exclaimed.

I was scared and freaking out. Drops of sweat poured off my forehead. I didn't know what to do to help her. I just crossed my fingers and hoped that she would be able to breathe again. I was looking at her feet and both of them flashed brown, then white, then bright blue. She was whipping her body around on the bed. *Please don't die! Please don't die!*

Her breath came back and she began gasping hard with a steady flow. All the colors had vanished and her skin had returned to normal. She jumped up and ran to the bathroom.

"GO!" Buzz shouted, in my right ear.

Right then, Buzz and I hauled tail out of the closet and zipped down the hallway. Echoing sounds came from the bathroom. She was puking her guts into the toilet. Moving fast, we flew down the steps, making our move for the front door. I was reaching for the handle when a nurse blurted out in a shrill voice, "BURGLARS!"

I yanked open the door and we took off running. As

we sprinted down the street, we heard the bells of a passing cable car. Just as it zipped by, we both leaped out and landed on the back rail, shooting down a hill, feeling the cool air brush against our faces.

Buzz and I panted like wild dogs and smiled. Without saying a word, we knew that our incredible adventure was finally over. Though my heart was torn, no money would end up in my pocket. But, tomorrow was a new day and, more than ever, I believed my future was bright. My old beat-up sneakers had stood on a floating launch platform in the Pacific Ocean with a space shuttle. That was enough proof for me that I had the talent to do something to save our Christmas tree farm. I had high hopes that something good could still happen—I just couldn't figure out what it might be.

CHAPTER TWENTY-TWO

Victory

As usual, Buzz barged into my room unannounced and tossed a baseball at my head. I snagged it with one hand—if I didn't, it would be lights out. I didn't want a black eye.

"Quit daydreaming. Let's play ball with the guys," Buzz said.

He trudged off, and I lazily got up from my cozy bed, laced up my sneakers, tossed on my San Francisco Giants baseball cap, and strolled from my room to begin the last week of my summer vacation. As I went through the garage to get my bike, I paused for a moment to look at my burned-up Commando, which reminded me of Titan. *Amazing,* I thought to myself how they resembled each other in perfect likeness.

My robot was lodged in the corner next to Dad's fried lawnmower. I chuckled as I remembered the day it had zoomed down the street, wiping out mailboxes, a prized rose garden, and a stop sign. *What a disastrous day that was,* I thought, shaking my head.

"What are you going to do with that thing?" Buzz asked, sitting on his bike.

"Go back to the old drawing board," I replied with confidence.

"Good luck," Buzz mumbled, pedaling away.

I jumped on my bike and rode down the street, feeling the soft breeze brush against my cheeks. Riding peacefully, I thought about everything that had happened during my summer vacation. Being reunited with my family had been a dream come true. I would never forget Mom and Dad, who had tears of joy flowing down their cheeks while they embraced me and Buzz at Fisherman's Wharf. The greatest relief had been discovering that Uncle Milo hadn't died in that vicious storm. After his boat had capsized, he miraculously landed on a populated island. They radioed the coast guard and searched all over the sea for me and Buzz—needless to say, they didn't have any luck finding us.

I glided around a corner, making my way down the home stretch to the ball field. I glanced up and stared at a jet cruising in the clear blue sky. It reminded me of the action-packed space shuttle ride I'd lived through. The splashdown had been the greatest thrill, the climax of the trip. It had been the ride of a lifetime, etched in my brain forever.

I focused ahead and sighed. It was gut-wrenching to dwell on the fact that we would end up losing our Christmas tree farm. My ambition to get the money was alive. I believed, even in the last inning, that I could somehow save the day and be the hero by hitting a grand-slam home run.

I remembered Dad announcing to me and Buzz just last week that the family business was fast coming to an end. Buzz, Mr. Tough-As-Nails, sank low into the couch, it being his first time to hear the news about the ugly situation. Tears trickled down his face, not a frequent Buzz event. It was a heartbreaking family moment. Never would I forget how Dad spoke, declaring the news in a gentle and humble voice. He scrunched his eyebrows in, creating a wave of wrinkles that lined his forehead, which translated to me that he was under great stress. Feeling great sorrow, I swallowed hard, just as I did when I heard the news the first time.

As I pedaled on, I thought of the word *hope*. The dictionary defined it as desire with expectation of fulfillment. That was what I felt every time the phone rang—my heart would race, hoping it was a toy company that was dazzled by the videotape I had sent out advertising *Aqua-Launch*, the first mini floating launch pad that could allow a model space shuttle to blast off from the water. *What kid wouldn't want this cool setup?* Someone would want to buy the rights to it and the money would be flowing in.

I continued my easy-going ride, reliving my action-packed adventurous summer vacation like it was a movie flickering in my overworked brain. I visualized the coin. I hadn't kept that coin with me since the adventure had ended; it was sitting safely in a box tucked away in my dresser drawer.

In my mind I could clearly see myself racing Buzz down the wooden dock that ended at Uncle Milo's huge yacht that had taken us deep into the Pacific Ocean. I closed my eyes for a few heartbeats, seeing the Viking treasure, only to have my heart rate increase rapidly as the perilous storm, that had left me and Buzz stranded on a deserted island, replayed itself in my head. Just thinking of that German shepherd dog and how I could have been history if it had gotten hold of me, sent a chill down my spine.

I ran over a rock and my eyes flashed open to see the ball field only a short distance away. I took my time, as I visualized Adam and how he changed colors and had Superman strength.

"Moon water," I muttered. "Incredible stuff. . . ."

There was no doubt in my mind that Adam had escaped and was somewhere on the planet—healthy, happy, and free. I knew that Adam and Julie would be together and had celebrated the miracle of having a second chance at life—all because of moon water.

Gently coming to a halt, I rested my bike along the dugout and trotted onto the diamond to see all the guys with their arms crossed.

"Hurry up, slow poke," a kid grumbled. "Next time call a taxi."

"Very funny," I shouted back, listening to a storm of laughter from all the guys.

I reached out for the bat Buzz was holding, took it, and dug in at home plate, ready to launch some homers.

"Could have been millionaires and saved our farm if you hadn't given the moon water to that girl," Buzz murmured bitterly from underneath his catcher's mask.

"Buzz, you're still a menace," I fired back, taking a huge swing and missing a blazing fastball thrown right down the middle of the plate by Lefty Mulligan.

"Could have been a rich one, too!" Buzz shot back.

Lefty zinged two more rocket-fast balls by me, and I was out.

"I'm up next," Buzz shouted from his squatted position.

Snatching up my Wilson glove, I ran out toward center field. It was a hot Saturday afternoon and I wiped pouring sweat from my forehead.

"Gatorade break!" Buzz announced from home plate. Everyone ran into the dugout, rushing for their favorite thirst quencher. I wasn't thirsty, so I took my position in deep center. Looking up at the sky, I continued to think back on my wild, wild summer.

Buzz and I had promised not to ever talk to anyone, except to Mom and Dad, about what had happened to us. Besides, who would have believed us anyway? We had seen the news a few days after we had gotten home, watching as reporters dug in and got the scoop on the space shuttle I had landed into the ocean.

I was on the edge of my seat that night, stunned to hear about the ship Buzz and I had been on. The reporter said it was a top-secret military vessel hidden deep in the Pacific Ocean by the United States Space and Defense Operations. It also had a secret launch complex for a classified mission in which the military was successfully launching space shuttles from the ocean to the moon. On the moon, top flight engineers and scientists had built a secret defense facility known as Area-X, and it was there space weapons for the future were being designed, built, and tested.

The President and Vice President, who were to view a space shuttle launch, were just hours away from boarding the ship when a mysterious explosion erupted. All military personnel were evacuated and no deaths came from the accident. It wasn't the unexpected explosion that terminated the secret space operation; it was terminated because leaks occurred when two young boys, lost at sea, discovered the program.

Just how those television reporters were able to put all the pieces together in a short period of time was impressive, I thought shaking my head. *Thank goodness the President and Vice President weren't on board.* From that day forward the images of that incredible adventure on that ship and floating launch pad never stopped going through my brain. Not only were those images fluttering in my mind, but not an hour went by that I didn't also think about Adam, wondering where he was and how he had escaped.

The guys hopped out from the dugout, finishing their Gatorade break, and were ready for another inning of baseball. Everyone charged the field, taking their positions as Buzz stepped up to the plate, took a hefty swing, and launched a home run that went over my head, flying over the fence behind me.

"I'll get it!" I shouted.

I hopped over the silver chain link fence and looked all over in the weeds for the ball. I searched for a long time, having no idea where it had rolled. Giving up, I decided to head back. When I turned around, my mouth flew open.

"Unbelievable, just unbelievable!" I choked.

Standing in front of me in blue jeans, dark sunglasses, and a leather jacket was Adam.

"Hey kid . . . looking for something?" Adam said, smiling, and flipped the baseball into my glove.

"You're free!" I exclaimed.

"And so are you. I just had to find you because I wanted to make sure you made it home alive."

"How did you find me?" I asked.

"I remembered the name of your small town," Adam said.

"Good memory."

"Anyway, I also want to say thank you for what you did. You kept your promise, and that means everything to me."

"How do you know I did?"

Adam turned around. A short distance away, I saw Julie seated on a motorcycle. She smiled and waved to me. I flashed her a thumbs up.

"How did you escape?" I asked.

"I forcibly took over the helicopter, gave the pilot a knockout punch, and made my way back to the mainland. When I got to San Francisco, I discovered that you somehow escaped and pulled it off. You saved Julie!" Adam said, excitedly. "Most kids would have cashed in on that moon water, but you didn't. Do you know what that makes you in my book?"

I froze, waiting for the answer.

"A hero," Adam declared.

I stood speechless, as a big grin inched across my face.

"EERRRICC! COME ON! HURRY UP!" the right fielder yelled at me.

"I've got to go," I said backing up. "But before I do, what happened to the moon water?"

"Fighting with the pilot, the helicopter went into a nosedive and the crate of moon water opened. All the vials smashed."

"No more moon water?" I asked.

"No more."

"What about your Hercules strength?"

"Wore off."

I gave Adam a wave and started to leave.

"I'll never forget you, kid," Adam replied.

I stopped and an idea flashed in my head. "Hey . . . could you sign this ball for me . . . sorta like a memento?"

Adam wore a bigger grin than mine. "I already did."

I flashed a thumbs-up and started to leave again when Adam said one last thing, "Hey, I have something for you." He reached into his leather jacket, pulled out a white envelope, and handed it to me.

"What is it?" I asked, puzzled.

"Just my way of saying thank you for what you did. Go ahead, open it."

Shrugging, I tore open the envelope like it was a birthday present. I ran my index finger along the seal and felt a piece of paper. I pulled it out, looked at it, and pure excitement raced through me!

"HOT DANG!" I shouted, dumbfounded at the sight of what I was holding. My hand shook, holding a check for ONE MILLION DOLLARS! My heart pounded like a thundering racehorse charging for the finish line at the Kentucky Derby.

"Is this real?" I choked, wide-eyed.

"Every zero of it," Adam said with a cool grin on his face. "Remember how much money I made being a stuntman?"

"A ton of it."

"Good memory. Anyway, I decided to split it with you for what you did."

Glowing, I raised my arms in victory!

"You deserve it, kid," Adam said. "I call it 'hero's

pay' for saving my girl and keeping your promise. Good luck and good-bye." He then saluted me and took off. I tossed him another thumbs-up, backpedaled a few steps, spun around, and raced as fast as my feet could fly back to Buzz.

"Look at all those zeroes!" I blurted out, sprinting through the weeds. I was so excited as I ran that I started to stumble over my feet. Catching my balance, I kept muttering out loud a zillion times, "Buzz is never going to believe this! Buzz is never going to believe this!"

I flew over the fence, looking at Buzz and the guys running to me. My heart was pounding, knowing somehow, someway, my million-dollar wish had finally come true. Even though I'd promised myself that I'd never say the word *wish* again, I was excited, so I let the thought linger for a moment longer. Something in the universe had made it happen! I looked back to see Adam and Julie, but they were gone. The only sign of them was the dust left by their motorcycle, which swirled and then drifted away in the wind.

Unable to think anymore, thrilled beyond belief about what had happened, I tried to express my feelings and emotions in words, only to find that I couldn't. I closed my eyes, took a deep breath, and counted to ten. Releasing the hot air, I opened my eyes, and two final words popped into my brain: *Happy Endings* . . . they were definitely the best words I could think of!